WITH A WAVE OF HIS HAND, ZANOS SET THE TREES AFLAME.

The two archers yelled in fear as they leaped from their hiding place. Even before they hit the ground, the Adept was on his feet, concentrating his powers. The killers' hearts stopped.

He concentrated again to extinguish the fires, just as Astra warned, "Behind you!"

Zanos spun and leaped aside as a ball of fire came hurtling at where he had been. The Adept who threw it was pressing his attack with more fireballs. Zanos stood his ground and deflected them, then tried to stop the bandit's heart. The other Adept clutched at his chest but resisted. They were locked in a struggle of powers when other bandits swept into the fray, swords swinging. But Zanos dared not move, couldn't let his concentration slip, or the other Adept would win out and kill them all!

Flight to the Savage Empire

Jean Lorrah
and
Winston A. Howlett

A SIGNET BOOK

NEW AMERICAN LIBRARY

NAL BOOKS ARE AVAILABLE AT QUANTITY DISCOUNTS
WHEN USED TO PROMOTE PRODUCTS OR SERVICES.
FOR INFORMATION PLEASE WRITE TO PREMIUM MARKETING DIVISION,
NEW AMERICAN LIBRARY, 1633 BROADWAY,
NEW YORK, NEW YORK 10019.

Copyright © 1986 by Jean Lorrah and Winston A. Howlett

Cover art by Segrelles

SIGNET TRADEMARK REG. U.S. PAT. OFF. AND FOREIGN COUNTRIES
REGISTERED TRADEMARK—MARCA REGISTRADA
HECHO EN CHICAGO, U.S.A.

SIGNET, SIGNET CLASSIC, MENTOR, PLUME, MERIDIAN AND NAL BOOKS
are published by New American Library,
1633 Broadway, New York, New York 10019

First Printing, March, 1986

1   2   3   4   5   6   7   8   9

PRINTED IN THE UNITED STATES OF AMERICA

Foreword

The entire *Savage Empire* series is dedicated to the person who got me into professional sf writing and then encouraged me to start my own series:

Jacqueline Lichtenberg

This book, of course, is also dedicated to Winston Howlett, who came up with the idea and the main characters, and did much of the preliminary drafting of the manuscript.

I would also like to thank the many readers who have sent comments about the first three books in the series; I hope you enjoy this fourth book in the *Savage Empire* universe.

If there are readers who would like to comment on this book, our publishers will forward letters to us. If you prefer, you may write to us at Box 625, Murray, KY 42071. If your letter requires an answer, please enclose a stamped self-addressed envelope.

All comments are welcome. I came to professional writing through fan writing and publishing, where there is close and constant communication between writers and readers. Thus I shall always be grateful for the existence of sf fandom, which has provided me with many exciting experiences, and through which I have met so many wonderful people—including the coauthor of this book!

Jean Lorrah
Murray, Kentucky

For my family, who sometimes encouraged, and the rest of the time knew that this was inevitable.

Winston Howlett
Calumet Park, Illinois

Chapter One

Shield smashed against shield. Metrius stumbled backwards, nearly falling.

Clavius pressed his advantage, sword battering away at Metrius' defense. Finally he found an opening, his sword slithering along the edge of Metrius' shield to gash his thigh.

As pain penetrated, Metrius sucked in a shocked breath and tried to strike back.

The crowd leaped to its feet, roaring encouragement.

The two evenly matched champions had been battling for close to an hour. Now, the long-awaited climax was at hand.

The ending could not come soon enough for Magister Astra. She was not in the stands, but huddled in the small medical treatment room beneath them, waiting for one gladiator or the other to be carried in with a grave or fatal wound. Here, for the eighth time today, she would either work frantically to save a life . . . or administer opiates to ease the last moments of a dying man.

In either case, she thought bitterly, *the punishment and pain are mine.*

For the hundredth time that day, the young woman wished she were anywhere else in the Aventine Empire—someplace without pain, suffering, or violence. But she could not escape her duty, any more than she could escape her Reader's talents.

No matter how hard she tried, she could not fully shut out the emotions of the people in the arena. They reeked with bloodlust, enjoying the match— she struggled not to be swept up in their fervor.

But worse than that, her inner vision put her in the very center of the life-and-death battle.

She tried to focus her powers away from the carnage, searching for something to concentrate on as the last match of the season ground to a close. This match—the main bout for which everyone had waited eagerly—was likely to end in death, not just injury. If she could find something to hold her full attention for a minute or two, perhaps she wouldn't feel the deathblow so sharply.

There. On the near sidelines, one man's thoughts stood out from the others'. Calm, rational, he shouted instructions to one of the gladiators. "Careful, Clavius—don't get careless! Keep your guard up!"

Of course—he was coaching Clavius, the soon-to-be victor.

Astra Read the man's exterior, and found herself "looking" at a tall, well-muscled man built like a gladiator himself. His rough-hewn face was crowned by tousled red hair. A slave from the northern isles.

No, she corrected herself as she looked further, *he's too well dressed for a slave. He must be a freedman . . . probably Clavius' owner as well as his coach.*

Suddenly her attention was torn from the red-haired man by a strange mental outcry—puzzlement mixed with fear. Involuntarily her focus changed to the center of the arena. Metrius lay sprawled on his left side, still losing blood, barely able to raise his sword. But the cry hadn't come from him.

It was *Clavius*!

He was trying to raise his sword to deliver the deathblow, but his muscles wouldn't respond!

He started to shake, not in fear, but in convulsions. His mind again cried out for help—then screamed as

Metrius, with his last strength, drove his sword up from the ground, piercing beneath the rib cage and into Clavius' heart.

The Reader screamed in empathic pain as she withdrew her mind from the scene, clutching her chest. She had felt her own heart stop for a moment, but now it beat all too rapidly.

Concentrating, she told herself the pain was not hers, and forced the sensation to subside as she brought her heart rate and breathing back to normal.

What happened out there? she asked herself. *It's as if the wrong man won!*

The roar of the crowd confirmed her thought. They were cheering Metrius, but their praise echoed Astra's astonishment. A few minds gleefully celebrated victory—but many people had lost heavily on the favorite.

Metrius managed to drag himself to his feet, and even those who had bet against him cheered wildly at his spirit. He limped a few paces, and then was lifted by his fellow gladiators. Their own medic pressed a clean cloth over his wound, and Astra Read that the worst of the bleeding had stopped. He could have his triumph before being brought to her for treatment.

Meanwhile, she Read two burly men carrying Clavius' body out of the arena, through the portal known as Loser's Gate. They would come down the tunnel to the medical station. Astra composed herself, the image of a competent Reader, ready to perform her last official tasks of the day.

But the stretcher-bearers didn't place the body on the examining table. In fact, they kept right on moving toward the exit, as though Astra did not exist.

"Stop!" she said sharply, and Read annoyance from both men as they complied.

"Nothin' you can do for this one, Healer," one of them said.

"Nothing except my job," Astra said firmly. "I must officially declare him dead, and you know it."

All day long she had been having trouble with these two men—muttered remarks about her competency while she worked on the wounded fighters, and looks of contempt when two of the gladiators died of their wounds. *It may be common knowledge that this duty is given as punishment to Readers who have displeased the Masters of their Academies*, she told herself, *but I've had enough of this riffraff treating me like a kickdog*.

But she said nothing, for she had been half sick all day from the athletes' pain. The stretcher-bearers couldn't have missed her paleness, and the sweat that broke out on her face when she forced herself to Read a man's agony to discover how to treat his wound.

But the very sensitivity which caused her misery at this task let her know no guilt—no one could have saved the two who died, not the most skilled healer at Gaeta.

This dead man did not disturb her—he no longer felt pain. The clean wound to the heart was indeed the cause of Clavius' death, but that was not what provoked her curiosity. She closed her eyes and concentrated, focusing her powers for a thorough scan of the dead man's organs.

She didn't find what she expected—a clot or broken vessel in his brain—but rather she discerned a strange substance in the gladiator's bloodstream. Barely a trace, so little another Reader might have missed it, but with Astra's sensitivity—

"Vortius, get out of my sight!"

The outburst cut across Astra's wide-open Reading like a thrown knife—but instead of shielding her mind, she widened her range to "hear" and "see" more.

At the sports arena, "Vortius" could only be Vortius the Gambler, a man who lived—richly—on the edges of both respectability and the law, profiting from the losses of others.

A man Astra loathed.

Yes, there he was—near one of the gladiators' entrances to the arena. He wore the clothes of an aristocrat, but had the demeanor of a street criminal. The man shouting at him was the one Astra had Read coaching Clavius. With the bearing of a fighter, he seemed about to pounce on Vortius . . . if the gambler weren't flanked by two large and ugly bodyguards.

"I can understand why you're upset," Vortius was saying with the obviously false sympathy guaranteed to infuriate the person it was turned on. "Clavius was your best fighter. A tragic loss for you, Zanos."

Zanos? Of course! Zanos the Gladiator, she realized. Even the Readers cloistered in their Academies knew of this magnificent champion. Two years ago he had retired undefeated, hailed as the greatest gladiator of the century. Now he had his own stable of gladiators and, judging by the wagering on the games, had been prospering.

Until today.

". . . losing so much gold must be doubly tragic," Vortius was saying as he hefted a heavy sack of coins. "It could have been avoided if you had accepted my offer."

"To become partners with you?" Zanos sneered. "Hah! I don't know what you did to Clavius to make him lose that match and his life, but—"

"I did nothing to him, Zanos," Vortius said, trying unsuccessfully to sound righteously indignant. "I didn't have to. Clavius did it to himself. Against your training rules, he sneaked off to a bordello last night."

Zanos' eyes widened. "You're lying!"

"Half a dozen people saw him at Morella's!" Vortius threw back at him. "You're a fool, Zanos, if you think you can impose your impotence on your men. It's a wonder Clavius could stand up today, let alone fight—with Morella's hellcats, I doubt he got much sleep!"

"And when you found out about it, you decided to help me not by warning me, but by betting against Clavius?"

Vortius shrugged. "I'm a businessman, Zanos, first and always." He shifted the sack of coins from one hand to the other. "If you and I had been partners yesterday, I could have seen that Clavius didn't violate your rules. My men would've kept him in his quarters."

Zanos let out a sound of disgust and walked away from Vortius, through Loser's Gate and down the tunnel. Vortius shouted after him, "He wasn't the only one of your men disobeying you, Zanos! You need my help to keep them in line, or you'll lose a lot more!"

"Aren't you finished picking over his bones yet, Reader?"

The stretcher-bearer's surly question brought Astra back to herself. She glared at him as Zanos swept into the room like a windstorm, radiating anger. The other men backed wordlessly away from the examining table as he stalked to it, demanding, "Why is Clavius' body still here?"

Astra stood her ground, but hesitated in her response. Even from the other side of the table, he towered over her like a giant. "Well, Reader?" he pressed.

"You are the owner of this gladiator?" she asked formally.

"Yes," he said curtly, "and I want his body decently buried before nightfall. What is the delay?"

"This man died from a sword thrust, all right," she replied, "but he shouldn't have lost that match. I Read traces of white lotus in his—"

"White lotus?" he echoed. "The dream drug? That's impossible! I don't let my fighters use drugs! Besides, white lotus isn't a stimulant—it's slow poison!"

"Indeed," Astra nodded. "Of all the deadly, habit-forming drugs to be found in the Aventine Empire, white lotus was the most insidious. She knew some of the idle rich played with this flavorless powder by putting it in wine and drinking their way to wild, "happy" dreams . . . and eventually forgot all else in life. The most severe cases ended up at the Gaeta hospital, where Master Readers used all their skills against the damage done to minds as well as bodies—for the substance also made the user highly susceptible to suggestion. Officially, the drug was illegal, but like many other illegal or unjust things, it flourished in the empire, especially in Tiberium.

"There is no way Clavius could have obtained white lotus!" Zanos insisted. "Morella's women might give themselves to a gladiator for the pleasure of it, but no one provides a slave with such an expensive drug—nor a gladiator he plans to bet on with such a dangerous one. I don't know what game you're playing, Reader, but you'd better forget it—and tell the same to your Masters!" *This one's just as corrupt as the others*.

Astra turned away from Zanos as he ordered the bearers to remove the body. His thought had struck her like a physical blow, but it was a kind of assault she'd grown used to. When the young Reader was upset or frightened, it was impossible for her *not* to Read the thoughts of others.

Something about this Zanos—besides his anger—frightened her very much. She couldn't argue with him—he must be very stupid not to realize that a debilitating drug that was very difficult to detect was exactly what one might give a gladiator one meant to bet *against*. Yes—dullness combined with great strength was a very dangerous and frightening mixture.

Metrius' trainer brought the victorious gladiator in just after Zanos left, and for a time Astra was occupied with cleaning and bandaging his wound. He would be fine—and after today's victory, with the winter to recover, would probably be a great favorite in the games next spring.

Then Astra was alone in the room again. Alone, as she had been for most of her life. Alone with the powers too strong for her to control, despite her years of training at the empire's finest Academy. The teachers had called her their finest pupil, but none of them could show her how to fully stop Reading, to completely shut out the world as even the least sensitive Reader could do.

She waited until the stadium and nearby streets were nearly empty before starting back to the Academy. The mental "noise" of a crowd was more than she could stand in her emotional exhaustion.

As the late-afternoon sun turned the streets crimson, Astra pulled her robe tighter against the chill autumn wind. There was some consolation in the knowledge that even if she received another punishment assignment, for the next few months it could not be to suffer the carnage of the games. Today's blood-sport matches had been the last of the season. In a week or so, the stadium's underground chambers would be open for wrestling matches—entertainment exclusively for the social elite and wealthy gamblers.

People like Vortius.

Her stomach tightened in anger. Vortius was responsible—albeit indirectly—for the ordeal she had endured today. Astra had passed him yesterday in the hallway as she was entering Portia's office. She had not Read him, nor Portia—but the old Master's face had betrayed annoyance, and Astra had asked sympathetically, "What was Vortius doing here? Trying to trick Readers into some nasty plot again?"

Reading other people's thoughts for personal profit was against the Reader's Code, but people like Vortius would do anything to get Readers into their power. There had been a huge scandal some six or seven years ago, when some Readers from the Path of the Dark Moon had been bribed or threatened to make them spy on other men's business.

Astra had expected Portia either to comment on Vortius' audacity in approaching the Master of Masters or to tell her to mind her own business. Instead, Portia had demanded, "What are you doing here?"

Before Astra could protest that Portia had sent for her, the old woman had flown into a rage, accusing her of spying. "Since you don't know what to do with your powers, I'll give you something to occupy them!" And Portia had assigned her to medical duty at the gladiatorial games.

It wasn't fair! Portia ruled the girls and women of her Academy with an iron hand, but that hand squeezed Astra much tighter than it did the others. No matter what the young Magister did, or how well she did it, she could never gain Portia's approval, or even a word of praise.

I'm held responsible for my mother's wrongdoing, punished for the shame she brought on the Academy, Astra thought sourly. *I thought once I became a Magister I'd proved myself. But nothing has changed. The Masters and the other Magisters still treat me as if I'm the one who violated the Reader's Oath.*

As she approached the Academy's iron gate, the place seemed more like a prison than her home, a place where she was—

—just as corrupt as the others—

Zanos' stinging thought came back to her, unbidden. The remark was not really surprising, for there was indeed corruption in the Reader system. Unguarded thoughts and unwanted bits of gossip had impinged on Astra all her life, but in recent years she had pieced together from them a picture of something sinister that began even within the Council of Masters, and spread throughout the empire.

That "something" involved Vortius, which explained why he was visiting Portia. Did the man dare attempt to apply his filthy pressures even on the Master of Masters? No wonder Portia had been upset.

Maybe that's why I was punished—not really for

anything I'd done, but because of something Vortius said. Something she was afraid I'd overheard.

Astra grabbed one of the bars of the gate and stood there for a moment, now feeling more than angry. Whatever was going on, she wanted no part of it. But the longer she remained in ignorance, the more vulnerable she would be to—to whatever disaster might be coming.

The gods have made me the most powerful Magister Reader in the empire's finest Academy, she told herself. *There must be a reason for it—it's not right that all I do is suppress my powers. Yes, they bring me pain—but they find things other Readers can't . . . like white lotus in that gladiator's blood. If I don't fight the corruption, am I not just as guilty as those who are spreading it?*

Not knowing exactly what she was looking for, Astra scanned the Academy's main building, seeking Master Portia. If she was cautious enough, and Portia was otherwise occupied, the old woman might not notice she was being Read.

Portia wasn't in her office. Neither was Master Marina, her assistant. Master Claudia was sitting at Portia's desk, her attention focused on the yellowed pages of an ancient book. Astra carefully withdrew without calling attention to herself. *If Claudia is in charge, neither Portia nor Marina is on the Academy grounds. Again.*

Unlike Portia, Claudia would not demand an explanation if Astra was late with her medical report. She could steal a little time to find out what was really going on.

But where to begin? She had no confidants, no informants—

Morella. Vortius claimed that Clavius had died in the arena because he went to Morella's last night. Astra had not been Reading for the truth of the man's statements, but it hadn't rung true—could Vortius have known about the drug?

Morella owes me a favor, Astra thought as she hurried away from the Academy. *Perhaps I can get her to repay it.*

The southeast quarter of Tiberium was called The Maze by those who knew it well, a neighborhood of taverns, theaters, and brothels. Sumptuous apartments belonging to people made wealthy by these trades lined some of the narrow streets, which denizens of the quarter roamed in gaudy finery. Here lived people of new wealth—those who might display silken robes . . . and dirty fingernails.

Here also roamed many of the more unsavory people of the city. Despite the chill, Astra was glad she was wearing her black Magister's cloak instead of her heavier gray one, for her position as a Reader would be respected even in this disreputable part of Tiberium. Without such indication, a woman who walked these streets alone risked insult, or worse.

Seven months before, she had walked through these same streets to Morella's House of Pleasure for the first time. Licensed and taxed by the government, the bordello required a monthly health inspection of its employees by a Reader. Like the gladiatorial games, it was a task given to a Reader who had fallen into disfavor with Portia. That time, Astra had argued with Portia, and knew she deserved the punishment duty. Still, she disliked it.

Morella hadn't made the job easy. A large, buxom woman of about fifty, she ran her establishment the way Portia ruled the Academy. But Astra had refused to be bullied into the superficial job other Readers must have done. She had thoroughly checked the fifteen prostitutes for communicable diseases or pregnancy—and then insisted on Reading Morella, even though she no longer "entertained."

It didn't take Astra long to find what the bordello owner was trying to hide: pain in her abdomen and opiates in her bloodstream. Further examination revealed not the cancerous tumor Morella had feared, but merely polyps which any surgeon could easily remove.

That good news brought tears of relief to Morella's eyes and a great change in her attitude toward Astra. After the operation and her release from the hospital, Astra had visited her often, both to check on Morella's recovery and to cultivate the only friendship she had been able to gain since becoming a Magister Reader. Morella was, Astra had to admit, closer to a motherly counselor than Portia had ever been to her.

So close had Morella and Astra become that Morella had called for Astra some three months ago, to help treat one of her women whom Astra had never met before.

"Clea worked for me for almost a year," Morella explained, "but she always complained that she didn't make enough money. She loves jewelry—or she did. She has nothing left now."

"What happened to her?" asked Astra, Reading the pale and silent woman on the bed. The bones of her face suggested that Clea had been beautiful, but now her skin was gray and taut, her face skeletal, her hands clawlike.

"Archobus lured her away," explained Morella. "He's an aristocrat who gambles with Vortius. He gave Clea all the silks and jewels she wanted—until he got tired of her. Then she became a hanger-on of Vortius' crowd down at his villa in the southlands . . . and someone addicted her to white lotus."

And that was how Astra came to recognize that particular taint in a person's blood.

"Morella," Astra said, "there's no herb I can give her, nothing that will cleanse the drug from her body. At the hospital at Gaeta, all the Readers can do for someone addicted, whether to opiates or to one of these rarer drugs, is to lock the person up while his body purges itself."

"I know that," said Morella. "That is why Clea came to me. She wants me to restrain her—but she's so weak, Astra! Can she survive?"

Although painfully thin, Clea was still in reasonably good health. Her heart was sound, and amazingly she had no disease. "Yes, I think she can survive," said Astra, "but we should take her to the infirmary at the Academy, where better healers than I—"

"No!" said Morella. "She trusts me. She would see it as betrayal if I turned her over to strangers. I don't suppose you know much about drug addiction, Magister . . . but I see it often here in The Maze. Clea has found the determination to cleanse the drug from her blood—but it will not last once the pain begins. And afterward . . ."

"Afterward, she is likely to go right back to the drug at the first disappointment in her life," said Astra. "At Gaeta, too, people go through all that suffering, only to return to their drugs."

"Because there are always vultures waiting to control them," said Morella. "But Clea will be safe with me. You've examined my girls often enough to know I will have no drugs here."

The woman on the bed groaned and opened her eyes. "Morella!" she gasped on a wave of pain. Astra gritted her teeth against it.

Morella took Clea's hand. "I'm here, child. You're going to be all right."

The young woman's eyes slowly focused on Astra. "You . . . you are the healer?"

"Yes."

"Morella says . . . you can be trusted. Please— please help me."

Astra took Clea's other hand, Reading her determination to be free . . . and the reason for it. Although the identities of the people were obscured in a drug-induced haze, the content of the scene that had sent Clea fleeing from her life of luxury was clear.

It was not the first time she had been given in-structions just when the white lotus had taken over her will. Without hesitation, she had read docu-ments belonging to various lovers, and reported their contents. She had stolen keys, delayed men from appointments, and even deliberately destroyed a mar-riage. Everything had seemed to be her own desire—until the day when someone had handed her a vial of poison and instructed her to seduce another man, then slip the poison into his wine.

Perhaps the man who instructed her had mis-judged the timing of the weakness of will white lotus produced, or perhaps Clea's tolerance had so in-creased that the dose was not enough to make her accept such an order. Whatever the reason, she had resisted—had run away, back to Tiberium, where she could disappear into The Maze. There she had sold her jewels, and her body, for drugs to feed her craving and erase the memory of that command to murder—that command she had almost obeyed out of mindless compulsion!

Finally, she had realized that she could not escape the memory . . . and that unless she escaped the drug her body craved more and more of, one day she might be willing to kill just as she had robbed and exploited.

And so she had come to Morella, the one person in The Maze she could trust.

Now she turned to the older woman. "Morella—please. Lock me up. It's starting. I'll run away if I can escape!"

"The door is locked, child," Morella assured her. "Phaeru has the key, and she will not open the door unless *I* tell her to."

As the hours passed, Clea's resolve melted as she had foretold. She screamed and raved, reviling Morella and Astra, threatening, even trying to climb out the tiny window that would not have admitted a cat.

Astra suffered the cramps, the vomiting, the stabbing pains along with her, sweating and shaking as time and again she helped Morella restrain their wild patient and force herb tea into her to combat dehydration.

It seemed to go on forever, until Clea passed out one last time, and then drifted into true sleep. So did an exhausted Astra, to be awakened some time later by Morella. "Come. Look."

Clea was awake, weak but without pain—and her mind was clear and under her own control. Her eyes glowed in her ravaged face as she took Astra's hand. "Thank you," she whispered, tears of weakness coursing down her cheeks. "May all the gods bless you, Magister!"

To the pleasant surprise of both Morella and Astra, Clea remained free of her addiction. She regained her beauty, and was once again one of Morella's favorites. She also regained her love of jewelry, especially rings—and when her customers found out what pleased her, she soon had a ring for every finger—and even some for her toes!

The incident with Clea had brought Astra and Morella closer yet, but even so, Morella wouldn't be happy to see Astra at her door after sundown on this last day of the blood-sport season; a Reader in the place during business hours would send customers scurrying away! Aware that she was racing the setting sun, Astra increased her pace. She Read ahead before she turned the corner, not that she expected to encounter another Reader in this part of Tiberium—

To her surprise, the scarlet of a Master Reader's cloak met her inner vision. He was male, and very old, accompanied by a boy who hobbled on a wooden leg. The boy was a Reader in training, wearing a plain white tunic under a brown wool cloak. Neither he nor the old man was Reading.

They did not have to; it was Astra's duty to avoid meeting the Master Reader, male to female, as he outranked her. Even if she were a Master herself, his age would make it the duty of every female Reader short of Portia herself to keep out of his way.

But what is he doing here? she wondered.

Astra realized that if she remained where she was, the two male Readers might see her when they reached the street corner. She ducked into a narrow passageway between buildings, annoyed at being thus delayed.

She knew who the Master and the boy were: Master Clement, formerly of the Adigia Academy on the northern border, and one of his students. Astra let her annoyance take the form of Reading them—after all, they were talking openly.

"But Torio was my *friend!*" the boy was protesting. "He wasn't a traitor. I know it!"

"Although that is possible, Decius," said the old man, "for your own safety you must not say so. No talk of Torio or Master Lenardo, no matter what the other boys say."

"But—"

"You are old enough to know that sometimes it is best to keep silent—and that includes Reading. *Especially* Reading. Nothing is accomplished by defending Lenardo or Torio. Suspicion already falls on their friends."

They were talking about the traitor Lenardo, the renegade Reader who had turned against the Aventine Empire and now styled himself a lord among their enemies, the savages! Astra had heard that he had learned the savage sorcery, and could perform their vile tricks himself.

The old man and the boy reached the corner . . . and turned into the street Astra had been walking. This she had not expected. But the narrow passage she had taken refuge in paralleled the street she had meant to take. Time was flying, and the wind was less strong in here, so she turned and hurried along the alley, pressing herself against the wall to get past a cart.

Obviously, Master Clement feared that the boy Decius would be branded a traitor if he defended Torio. Torio *had* been a traitor, Astra knew, but she also understood adolescent loyalties. When she was ten or twelve, she would have said or done anything to defend Helena, the only true friend she had ever had in the Academy. Helena was nearly four years her senior, and a weak Reader, but their differences hadn't prevented them from becoming close.

When Helena had failed to pass her test for the rank of Magister, Astra had taken it upon herself to plead with Portia for Helena to be retested. But the Master of Masters had refused to listen, and Astra had been separated at age twelve from Helena, who had been as dear to her as any sister. Furthermore, Portia had punished Astra for trying to help Helena by forbidding her the Academy's musical entertainments for two months.

Had she been a mere spectator, Astra could simply have Read the entertainments from her own room. But she was a performer, skilled enough with her lute to be a professional musician were she not a Reader. So she had practiced alone, and brooded— and never again formed a close friendship, knowing that most of the other students either envied her strong powers or shunned her because of her mother.

Morella's place was only two streets away now, and Astra speeded her steps. Up ahead, the passageway was blocked by empty scaffolding, but Astra Read that she could walk beneath it. She began to thread her way through—

The earth shook! Astra was flung to her knees, thrown against one of the support rods. Pain lanced through her right shoulder, her scream drowned by the rumblings all around her. This was not another of the frequent tremors of the past few weeks—it was a full-fledged earthquake!

Astra gripped two crisscrossing rods as the quake's ferocity increased. The structure groaned, and she could feel the metal's strain as well as Read it. The whole thing could collapse on her!

Somehow she pulled herself to her feet, but it was all she could do to stay on them. The ground rippled like ocean waves. As the scaffolding's groans became a death rattle, the Reader closed her eyes and braced herself, ready to leave her body in the face of serious injury or—

Powerful hands grabbed hers, pulling her free of the rods. A thick arm squeezed her diaphragm as she was lifted off her feet and through the iron forest just as it was collapsing. She and her would-be rescuer fell to the cobblestones, his body sheltering hers. Astra heard wood and metal crash thunderously near their heads . . . but they weren't touched.

The tremors were subsiding, as was the dust that had been flung up all around them. Astra breathed a prayer of thanks to all the gods as her savior slowly stood, tall and broad-shouldered. He reached down and easily pulled her to her feet, but still she looked far up into clear blue eyes set in a granite-carved face—a pleasant face despite its scars. A rough-hewn face crowned by tousled red hair.

Zanos the Gladiator.

"Are you all right?" he asked with a smile. Something in his deep voice sent a shiver down her spine.

"Except for a few bruises, yes . . , thank you," she heard herself reply. "It's a miracle we weren't crushed—"

Recognition finally lit his eyes. "You're the Reader I met in the stadium this afternoon, aren't you?" he asked softly. "Magister . . .?"

"Astra."

"I'm sorry for the way I acted today," he said. "I was upset at the death of Clavius . . . and at what his death has cost me. Later I realized you had to have been telling me the truth about the white lotus."

Astra said nothing, surprised at the unexpected apology.

"I'd like to talk with you," he said. "Can I escort you to wherever you're going?"

"My errand . . . wasn't important," she stammered. Thanks to the quake, Morella would be putting her place back together now, in no mood to answer questions. "It can wait until tomorrow. I must get back to my Academy—Readers will be on call to locate people buried in the earthquake damage and to treat the injured."

She turned to head back up the passageway—and found the wreckage of the scaffolding blocking her way.

"Allow me, Magister!" Zanos said as he swept her up in his arms. Startled by his boldness, she was still groping for words of protest after the gladiator had easily carried her over the debris and set her on her feet.

"Do you always give such 'help' to people?" she asked disapprovingly.

"Only to my friends." He smiled as he took her arm and began to lead the way. "I'll come with you—there may be other places like this. I'll help you back to your Academy, and you tell me how Clavius got that white lotus. He certainly didn't have money to pay for it."

As they walked, Astra collected her thoughts. "You didn't give me the chance this afternoon to tell you exactly what I found. There was only a *trace* of white lotus in Clavius' blood. If he used the drug regularly, he could not have had any in the past few days."

Zanos nodded. "Everybody in the stadium was watching the match, but I was concentrating on Clavius. He had a habit of dropping his guard when he got overconfident. But his actions just before he died *could* have been like those of someone craving white lotus. . . ."

"Like an addict who had been deprived of it," Astra mused, "and was just beginning to become

irrational. Yes, that would make sense . . . provided
Clavius was taking only small amounts."

"I don't think he was 'taking' it," Zanos insisted.
"I've been in the games for a long time, Magister.
Athletes are sometimes stupid enough to take drugs
they think will help them win. Painkillers, to participate despite an injury. Stimulants. But white lotus is
not something a gladiator would take willingly—it
does nothing at all to improve performance, and
taking it for happy dreams means the risk of having it
wear off at a crucial moment, leaving the user
helpless."

"Then—?" Astra prompted.

"Somebody drugged my man—or addicted him to
the drug and then used him against me. Maybe he
was supposed to throw the match today and refused—
and his supplier cut off his drugs." He looked down
at her, his eyes earnest. "I do not want to think
Clavius was disloyal to me . . . and now there is no
way to question him."

"The amount in his bloodstream was very small,"
said Astra. "He could not have been taking it for
long. You could be right that it was slipped to him
without his even knowing it. It's tasteless."

Zanos nodded. "Oh, yes—there's nothing unusual
about someone buying a gladiator a cup of wine.
Clavius won four days ago; those who had won on
him bought him so much wine at the celebration that
he passed out. The drug could have been slipped to
him then."

"But by whom?"

"I don't know. I thought you might."

Astra caught flickering images of various faces from
Zanos' mind. All of them were unknown to her,
except one—the face of Vortius.

"Do you think your other men are in danger,
Zanos?"

"Good question," he replied grimly. "Fortunately,
I have ways of finding out. Perhaps I don't know

everything that goes on in The Maze, but I keep informed. I live near here, you know," he said, suddenly changing the subject. Astra had expected him to ask her to Read his men. Strange. What was he afraid she would find?

"Let me show you my house," Zanos continued smoothly. "Should you need it, you will know where you can always find help in this part of town."

Astra did not miss the hopeful tone in his voice, and Read his intention as sincere—yet he had adroitly steered away from the obvious. She reassessed her earlier opinion of him as stupid, but what was he hiding?

Zanos' home was a small villa, the most impressive dwelling in the area. "I didn't know that a retired gladiator could live in such grand style," she commented.

Zanos gave a short, rueful laugh. "I may soon lose this 'grand style' . . . the villa, my fighters— everything. I lost a lot of money today, and if certain people have their way I could lose a lot more." An angry look crossed his face, and Astra suppressed a shiver—she couldn't Read his thoughts at that moment.

Zanos' pleasant smile suddenly returned. "Come on," he said, taking her arm again. "It's too cold to stand out here."

"Don't you want to see what damage the earthquake did to your house?" she asked.

"My servants will clean it up. That house is very well built—at most, the quake broke a few dishes."

But many buildings were not so well constructed. As they made their way along the street, they came to a spot where a ramshackle apartment building had collapsed. People were digging furiously in the rubble, women weeping as they tried to drag broken beams off the pile.

"Magister!" cried a man as he heaved part of a wall into the street and turned to find someone in Reader's robes. "Oh, Magister—tell us—are they alive?"

Astra didn't need the women to converge on her, crying, "Our babies! Our children!" for she could Read four children inside the house—alive but trapped.

"Yes," she told the mothers, "they're alive—but we've got to get them out. It's no use trying to get at them this way. They've fallen through to the cellar, and the rubble could collapse on them. Come around to the back. Zanos, please—"

He added his formidable strength to that of the other man as they heaved debris out of the stairwell leading down into the cellar. Hearing them, the children began to stir, the youngest to scream and the others to cry in terror.

Their mothers called to them, "It's all right! We're coming," but the children either couldn't hear over their own cries or were too frightened to be comforted by nothing but voices.

It was dark where the children were, and when they tried to move they encountered hard, sharp objects. One little boy of perhaps five tried to stand, and gashed his head on something piercing the trash above him. Blood flowed into his eyes, and he cried even louder.

The two women tried to squeeze past the men as soon as they had an opening into the cellar, but Astra cried, "Wait! Be careful! All that stuff could come down on them!"

"I'll get them," said Zanos, and somehow levered his huge body through the opening they had created. In a moment he handed out the screaming baby into its mother's eager arms, then the bleeding, crying boy.

Astra examined the wound, assuring the mother that it was nothing serious, the child more frightened than hurt.

Zanos, meanwhile, was trying to maneuver two little girls into position as they hindered him and one another by trying to climb out on their own. "Mama!

Mama!" they shouted, scraping knees and elbows on
the debris and shoving each other—

"Here now," said Zanos, "let me lift you—"

But just as he captured one of them and handed
her out to her mother, the rubble shifted, knocking
him down on top of the other child.

Both mothers and the three freed children began
to scream in earnest, their panic taking hold of Astra,
who was making no attempt to avoid Reading. For a
moment she stood shaking, her brow sweating, her
heart racing—and then she forced herself to take
hold as she Read Zanos pinned under the debris, but
still sheltering the child. Somehow, he had managed
to hold the roof of rubble up with his own strong
shoulders, instead of allowing it to knock him down
to crush the girl beneath him.

Astra and the man beside her began hauling everything they could reach off the pile. "Hang on,
Zanos!" she cried. "We'll get you out!"

She could feel the strain on his back—even a
gladiator's strength could not hold that weight for
long.

Finally they uncovered his head and arms, spread
to hold the debris off the child. When Astra reached
for his hand, he said, "No! Reach under me—pull
the child out!"

When the man did so, the girl reached eagerly for
his hands and was hauled to safety.

Zanos sank to his knees beneath the weight of
wall, floor, and furniture. Astra Read total weariness
in his overstrained muscles, as if at that moment he
could not even climb to his feet unassisted.

By this time other people had gathered, and they
quickly dug Zanos out, unhurt, although covered
with dust. "Zanos!" somebody exclaimed, and then
the people he had helped began to thank him, while
Astra wondered if he was going to be able to stay on
his feet.

The children were carried into a neighboring house,

and the couple who lived there, insisted, "Come in, come in—rest for a spell. Zanos the Gladiator. An honor!"

"Aye," said the mother of the injured boy as she smoothed his hair, "you'll tell your children about this, Borius. You was rescued by the greatest gladiator of all time!"

Zanos sank down on a pallet on the floor—the few chairs were hard wood. These were poor people, but they shared what they had. The woman showed the two now homeless mothers where to put their children to bed, then brought Zanos a mug of hot soup. Soon he was leaning against the wall, taking an interest in the bustle about them.

After assuring the women that all the children needed was to have their cuts and scratches washed, Astra turned to Read Zanos again, and found him recovering quickly. The ready grin was back as he listened to the owner of the house telling everybody who would listen, "Zanos the Gladiator! I seen him from the cheapest seats in the arena, and now he's in my own house! Remia! Open that cask of ale—"

"No—please don't," said Zanos. "The soup was all I needed, really. Thank you. Save everything else to help you help your neighbors."

Astra could Read his envious surprise at how these neighbors so readily shared their meager worldly goods. In his world it was dog eat dog—and a favor meant something expected in return.

The man ignored Zanos' protests, and soon put mismatched cups of ale into his hand and Astra's, saying, "Remember the day you won your freedom, Zanos? You was the best ever—we all said it. I won ten coppers on you that day—though Gromius said nobody could beat *three* of the best gladiators in one afternoon!"

"The gods were with me," Zanos replied.

Astra remembered—the whole city had talked of nothing else for days. She hadn't been there, of course, but she had heard that all three opponents were considered "unbeatable," yet Zanos had dispatched them one after another. As a reward for a show such as Tiberium had never seen before, the Emperor himself had granted Zanos his freedom, and the whole city had celebrated as if it had happened to each and every one of them personally.

Such was the impact of this strange man. It seemed instinctive to like him—but still something about him disturbed her. When he caught her eyes on him, he scrambled to his feet. "We must get you back to your Academy, Magister." And he would brook no argument against walking with her all the way, although she could Read that his body ached with the strain he had put it through to hold up that collapsing floor.

He left her at the Academy gates, and headed back the way he had come. As she watched him disappear around the corner, Astra shook her head in puzzlement. "It's a miracle we weren't crushed," she had said to him after the earthquake. And then he had saved those children—another miracle? Did the gods look with special favor on this man? Had the gods brought him into her life this day? Strange feelings stirred within her, and her memory replayed, uninvited, the feel of his strong arms lifting her—

No! she told herself firmly. *I am a Magister Reader, virgin-sworn. No man has a place in my destiny.* Certainly not that strangely compelling ex-gladiator.

"A *Reader*?" the old woman asked, appalled. "Have you gone mad?"

Zanos shook his head, fighting the confusion of fatigue. "What did you expect me to do? I saved her life. You always say life should be sacred, even to one who has killed so many in the arena. When the earthquake started, I just saw somebody in trouble. I didn't think about the color of her cloak—"

"Or consider the danger!" Serafon countered. "She

might have Read you—might have discovered your
secret! Indeed, she may be Reading for you at this
very moment, bringing the city guards to arrest you!"

"Serafon, she's not like that!" Zanos protested,
although he couldn't explain why he believed that
Astra *wasn't* just like any other Reader, constantly
spying. Before Serafon could ask, he squatted down
to her seated level and said gently, "I protected us.
Once I realized she was a Reader, I led her from the
temple area so cleverly she never realized I wanted
her away from here."

"You think you could fool a Reader?"

"She had no reason to suspect anything," he explained. "I apologized for shouting at her at the
arena today, told her stories—I kept her mind so busy
she had no time to think about Reading where I had
come from."

They were in an anteroom of the Temple of Hesta,
the goddess of the harvest, whose high priestess
Serafon was. She was a woman in her late fifties,
dressed in the beige-and-orange robes of her calling.
Her iron-gray hair was bound with bands of gold.
Her bearing was regal, but her concern for Zanos
was as clear as if he could Read her.

"This was the same Reader who discovered white
lotus in Clavius' blood," she continued. "What if she
suspects you know more about it than you admitted
to her?" Her eyes drifted to the shrouded corpse on
the nearby table. "You were his owner. You should
have known every facet of his life and training. She
could have been in that alleyway to spy on you—she
might think you're involved in the drug trade."

Zanos let out a derisive snort. "The Readers don't
care about drugs in the empire! If they used their
powers where it really mattered, there wouldn't be
any white lotus in Tiberium. They're paid to look the
other way, just like the city guards."

"I'm sure some of them are," Serafon conceded,
"but certainly not all of them. This Astra is a Magis-

ter, not a Master. She's young, maybe idealistic. Those Readers who are corrupt can't take just anyone into their confidence—they don't want to split the wealth too many ways, for one thing. And for another—"

"I know." It was the same reason Zanos and Serafon dared not try to identify others like themselves. "If the wrong person found out, their secrets could be made public before they could silence him . . . or her."

Serafon nodded. "Astra might be free of the corruption. If she found the drug in Clavius' blood, she must be a very thorough Reader—all she was assigned to do was verify that he was dead. Any Reader sent to do that job is not a highly regarded one, and most would have done only what was necessary. She sounds like an idealist.

"The Readers' Academies are much like this temple, Zanos—we have students and young priestesses who seek to ingratiate themselves with their elders. So, if Astra's youth makes her idealistic, and if she would like to get into the good graces of her superiors—"

"She might very well turn me in," Zanos reluctantly agreed, "*if* she suspected the truth. Serafon, I can't explain it, but I somehow don't think she would do that. If she suspects me of dealing in drugs, she won't act without evidence—and since I don't, she won't find any. Besides, if she had done what you fear, surely the city guards would be here by now. We're not in any immediate danger."

"If they're not waiting at your house," Serafon warned. "Zanos—don't risk everything on your hunch about this Reader. Stay away from her."

"You and I risk everything every day we stay in this land," he reminded her as he stood to stretch his legs. "We should have left the moment I won my freedom. The longer I stay here, the more danger there is from people like Vortius. He seems determined to take everything I have. Astra may be able to help me get the information I need to fight him . . . so I won't have to take more direct action."

"Zanos." Serafon's quiet tones forced him to look her in the eye. "Is that what you'd really like to do? Kill Vortius?"

He restlessly paced the tiny room, trying to sort out his thoughts. "It would be direct and clean. Serafon, I'm not a schemer like Vortius. But no, I don't want to kill him—or anyone else who has not agreed to the risk in honorable combat. Vortius chose to make us enemies, not me. For more than two years I've honored your wishes, because he is the son of your close friend. But friend or no, you don't dare tell her the secret you and I share."

Serafon replied grimly, "It has been more than a generation since I fled the southlands, but I remember the fear. More than that, I remember the temptation to kill—the desire to kill anyone who might prove a threat, should he or she learn about my gift—"

"Gift?" Zanos echoed. "It's a curse!"

"That curse enabled you to win every gladiatorial contest you've fought, and to do much good in secret. With such power comes equal responsibility, Zanos. Right now, you are feeling the weight of that responsibility."

The gladiator stopped pacing, searching for words to continue the argument, but fatigue was rapidly overtaking him. Serafon's wisdom had saved his life countless times, but sometimes his fighter's instinct outweighed any wisdom.

"Zanos," Serafon continued quietly, "you're a fighter, but you're not a murderer."

"No?" he asked. "I'm not so sure. Sometimes I see the faces of my opponents in my dreams—accusing me of killing them with unfair strength. At other times I feel their blood on my hands, blood that will never wash off." He stared down at his palms, then closed them into tight fists. "I hate this empire, Serafon. I hate them for enslaving me, and for what they made me do to stay alive. Most of all, I hate them for this mockery they call freedom—"

Serafon now stood before him, gently cupping her hands around his clenched fists, as though trying to draw the anger from his spirit. He could see his anguish reflected in her eyes.

"All I've ever wanted is to go home to Madura," he whispered. "To go home—and take with me anyone who lives in chains or in fear, and wants to breathe free air."

"Yes, Zanos, I know." Her left hand gently touched his face. "It is a most noble dream, but one that can come true only if you move with careful steps. Rash action will only bring you grief."

He nodded agreement—even though it was more that he was too tired to argue further than that he fully agreed. He needed at least one more season in the arena to pull together the money and connections required to make his dream a reality. One more year—would it really be murder to rid Tiberium of a man who threatened a plan that would help so many people?

As if she knew his doubts, Serafon said, "Zanos, please . . . leave Vortius to me. I have ways of influencing him that you do not know."

The strength of his anger was gone. "I'll do it your way," he agreed, "for the time being. But if Vortius forces a confrontation, I won't wait for your advice. He's not taking any more of my money—or my men," he added, glancing at the brown sheet covering Clavius' body.

Watching him, Serafon said quietly, "I understand," and left the room. He knew she was going to summon the temple workers to take the body for burial in Slaves' Field, amid a thousand other unmarked graves.

A thousand leagues from the homeland Clavius

never even got to see. "I'm sorry, my friend," Zanos whispered. "I failed you twice today—in the arena, and here in the temple. I can't believe you accepted that drug deliberately. You wanted to gain your freedom in reality, not in dreams. At least you are free now, Clavius. The gods have answered your prayers in their own way—but it was not the way I intended."

"You look as if you *crawled* back from the arena!" The voice that cut across Astra's thoughts could belong only to Magister Tressa, her closest rival for the Academy's honors. Tressa of the night-black hair and fierce dark eyes. Tressa of the deadly tongue. Tressa, who always knew everyone else's business, but was never caught violating the Reader's Code. Tressa was always in trouble, always pulling punishment duty—yet never doing anything quite bad enough to get herself transferred to a lesser Academy. Especially since her wide-ranging talent as a Reader had her tagged, as was Astra, as a potential future Master.

Astra threw a muttered greeting over her shoulder and tried to get away from this irritant, but Tressa caught up with her and pretended not to realize that Astra did not want her company.

"You don't seem to have any injuries," Tressa said as she scanned her. "Why did it take you so long to get back? What were you doing?"

"Finding some children trapped under a collapsed house," Astra replied truthfully.

But Tressa wasn't satisfied. "Wasn't that Zanos the Gladiator with you at the gate?"

Astra said nothing, merely enforced her mental shields and kept on walking toward Portia's office.

"Such an interesting man," Tressa went on. "I've spoken to him at the stadium. He's so . . . beautiful, don't you think? Like a wild animal, all that strength—is he the reason you're so late?"

"I didn't know you pulled so many punishment

assignments at the arena," Astra returned. "How many times have you angered Portia? A dozen times? A hun—"

Astra stopped in midsentence as a mental scream tore through her. Tressa must have "heard" it also, for her face reflected the anguish Astra felt.

Astra bolted for the door to Portia's office, Tressa on her heels. They burst in to find Master Claudia sitting at the desk with her face buried in her hands.

"Master Claudia?" Astra approached carefully. "Are you all right?"

The middle-aged woman slowly lowered her hands and looked up at both Magisters with an expression of horror. Astra became aware of running footsteps in the corridor, as other Readers converged on the office, drawn by the scream.

Claudia said in a choked voice, "I just received word from Master Portia. Master Quantus, head of the Palonius Academy, died suddenly tonight."

Grief-stricken reactions filled the room, a maelstrom of emotions that—for one terrible moment—threatened to drown Astra. But it subsided quickly, for none of the other women here knew Master Quantus personally—it was merely that one of their own was gone, and as Readers, they shared the grief of his fellows who truly mourned.

But as the wave of overwhelming grief subsided, it was replaced for Astra by a sudden anguish—mixed with fury.

As she closed her eyes, a single word softly crossed her lips, so gently that it was lost in the mourning sounds of the other Readers: "Murder!"

Chapter Two

By the time Zanos got home from the temple, he could do nothing but fall into bed and sleep. For some time he slept the dreamless sleep of exhaustion, but eventually his soul retreated into his favorite dream—the dream that had sustained him through all the years of his captivity.

He stood on the deck of a northbound ship, staring at the waters ahead as the blue sky slowly turned to a familiar iron gray. The air grew cool and crisp, and green islands appeared on the horizon, snow-capped mountains rising to greet him and his friends.

Above them, white birds with black-tipped wings circled the ship, and he pointed them out to Astra as she came up to him and lovingly slipped her arm around—

NO! Suddenly he was sitting up in bed, surrounded by darkness, hearing nothing but his own rapid breathing. "By Mawort—!" he swore, but broke off. He didn't really believe in the gods, not even the warrior god to whom his life was dedicated.

Serafon is right, he thought. *Why am I dreaming of a Reader in such terms?*

He didn't know, as he sat sweating in the darkness, which Astra terrified him more: the Reader who might discover his secret . . . or the woman who had in two brief encounters impressed him as no other woman ever had. Against his will, her face

appeared in his mind, mature yet childlike, with
beautiful features that reminded him of one of
the temple statues. When she had smiled at him
after the earthquake— He wanted to see that smile
again.

And I will, he told himself. *She is part of my
destiny.* He had not slept long enough to recover his
strength, and drowsiness began to overtake him again.
But before he yielded, one last thought warned,
That destiny may be my destruction.

In the Academy the next day, Astra also struggled
with a sense of impending danger. She had agreed to
meet Tressa out of body.

Why? she demanded of herself, thoughts carefully
shielded. *Why did I trust her? She's no friend—never
has been. I've often wished she could be, since it
would have been safe....*

Had Astra and Tressa been friends, they would not
have had to fear separation. Readers who failed to
reach the top ranks were married off to other failed
Readers, to produce children with stronger talents,
in service to the empire. Consummating such marriages weakened those Readers' meager powers, and
birthing children sometimes destroyed a mother's
powers entirely. In all cases, she lost contact with
the girls she had grown up with.

Astra remembered the sad day when her friend
Helena was wed to Tranos, a total stranger. She was
there at her friend's request, as the bride's attendant. Just before the ceremony, the two young Readers had stolen a few minutes by themselves. Helena
had cried in Astra's arms, for the badge of the Dark
Moon had just been pinned on her.

Both girls looked on it as an unearned mark of
shame. But even though Astra could sympathize with
her friend and offer her comfort, she could not fully
appreciate Helena's turmoil. For Astra, there was no

fear of treading the Path of the Dark Moon. How could someone cursed with so much Reading power *not* pass the test for Magister?

Four years later, when her turn finally came, it was all Astra could do not to appear overconfident to the Masters who tested her—in fact, she had been careful not to show the full range of her powers that day, for in one so young they might pose a threat to ambitious members of the Council.

She had passed, of course—but although her incredible strength and range guaranteed her a place in an Academy for life, she had not achieved the control she would have to have before making the final step into the ranks of Masters.

That was where Astra eventually planned to be. She still had ten years until she reached the height of her powers; surely by then she would gain control. Once in the highest rank, she would be in the realm of *real* power—perhaps in charge of an Academy of her own. And one day, in the far future, perhaps she might sit in Portia's seat. Master of Masters, Head of the Tiberium Academy, adviser to the Emperor—why was she risking all that on Tressa's dare?

But when Astra had been ritually washing her hands and face in the temple fountain before the memorial service for Master Quantus, Tressa had come up beside her and whispered, "I have the same suspicions you do. Foul play!"

But Tressa had been closed to Reading, and Astra, despite the startlement Tressa's statement caused her, had managed—she hoped—not to broadcast to the other Readers. Those other Readers were already taking their places, and the sound of running water covered their voices as Astra whispered back, "What do you mean?"

"You know what I mean!" the other Magister insisted. "After the service, when we all go back to our rooms to meditate, meet me on the plane of privacy!" And she shook the water off her hands and stalked to her place at the back of the temple. Astra followed, deliberately letting herself be caught up in the ceremony so that her turbulent emotions would attract no attention.

If only no one had Read that conversation—

Astra had not been able to tell that anyone had, and she was certain she could catch any Reader spying on them as they left their bodies. They simply would not move to the plane of privacy if there was anyone Reading them.

By the time Tressa's mind touched hers, Astra was certain they were alone. She left her body, which she had carefully arranged on her bed so that nothing would cramp or cut off her circulation while her attention was elsewhere.

Wordlessly, they moved together to the plane of privacy. Not since her last meeting with Master Quantus had Astra come here, where no Reader could eavesdrop on their conversation unless that person had come out of body and passed over to this particular plane with them.

Just as she was admiring the smooth techniques Tressa had achieved, the other woman broke the spell with the tasteless remark, //I thought that memorial service would go on forever.//

Astra made no attempt to hide her irritation. //What do you want to tell me?//

//Why are you so upset? You act as if Master Quantus was a friend of yours.//

Tressa knew they could never have met in person, but she didn't know the rest. //He *was* a friend. Like me, he was a musician—and Master Thenea sent me to him on the plane of privacy when she couldn't answer my questions on musical theory. He was a great authority—and very patient with a less experienced musician.// He had also given Astra valuable lessons in how to ask those difficult questions with-

out alienating her own teachers who didn't know the
answers. //From what little contact I had with him,//
she added, //he impressed me as a good teacher and
a very kind, gentle person.//

//Perhaps,// Tressa said with the mental equivalent
of a shrug, //but that's not the kind of person Portia
lets into her inner circle.//

//What do you mean?//

//The Council of Masters has split into two factions: Portia and other heads of Academies against
the Masters who don't teach. Portia's group may be
smaller, but they are well organized and in constant
communication. The others are divided over changes
in the Reader system—trying to prevent further fail-
ures at the Magister level after the poor showings of
the past few years.//

//I know all that,// Astra told her. //Get to your
point.//

//Four Masters have died in the past eight months.
One after a long illness, one in a mysterious accident, one in an Academy fire—which could have
been deliberately set—and now Master Quantus.//

//He died of heart failure,// said Astra.

//Did you examine the body? He had something in
common with the other three who recently died: he
disagreed with Portia's new policy of retesting Magisters and Masters. Last month, he brought a formal
protest before the entire Council when one of his
staff members was reevaluated and placed on the
Path of the Dark Moon . . . and now he's dead.//

Tressa's suspicions were only too familiar, for Astra
had been refusing to make the same connections in
her own mind. They had been the source of her
reaction to the news of Quantus' death—but it would
not do to speculate about such matters, especially
with the Academy's most notorious gossip.

She yearned to share her fears with another strong
Reader, but it had to be someone she could fully

trust. And there was no such person, she realized sadly, in the whole of the Aventine Empire.

At her mental silence, Tressa urged, //Astra, it's time to put our differences aside. If Portia can retest and demote even Masters—and may be murdering some she can't—what chance have young Magisters like us got if we look like a threat to her?//

//What are you proposing, Tressa?//

//We must create our *own* secret faction—the way they did at the Adigia Academy. Don't pretend you haven't heard about Master Lenardo and his students— first Galen went over to the savages, and then Lenardo followed. He came back for another student, Torio—and nobody's sure whether Master Clement can be trusted anymore.//

It was all Astra could do to keep Tressa from Reading her memory of Master Clement and that boy—Decius—walking through The Maze just before the earthquake. Were they plotting against the empire, afraid to talk within the walls of their own Academy?

After all, Lenardo had been exiled as a traitor for openly declaring that the Aventine Empire should seek peace with the Adept Lords who ruled the lands of the savages—the same savages who could set fires with the powers of their minds, throw thunderbolts, or stop someone's heart with a glance. They pushed back the walls of the empire, enslaved the citizens of the lands they captured, and killed any Readers they discovered. Everyone had expected Lenardo to meet the same fate—but he hadn't.

Not long ago the traitor had secretly returned to the empire, entered this very Academy, and faced Portia herself. Astra had seen a tall man with a beard and long hair, but at the time she had had no idea who he was. Soon enough the rumors had started flying—rumors Astra, of all people, could not shut out of her consciousness.

Some said that Lenardo had tried to twist Portia's mind, using the same Adept sorcery that his captors had used on him. If he had influenced Portia, though, it had been only briefly—she had raised the alarm that very night. Lenardo had fought clear of the city, stealing away one of his former students—a blind Reader named Torio—but the boy had been killed at the border.

Border security was tightened, but people lived in fear of what the savages might try next. What if Tressa was right? What if savage Adepts were indeed slipping in and out of the empire at will? This was no time for Readers to be disputing with one another!

//You want us to turn traitor?// she demanded of Tressa.

//No! I'm saying we can borrow their *methods*. Astra, just think about it—the Aventine Empire has already lost half its territory. Lenardo has formed an alliance with the savages and even learned their Adept powers. Our only safety was that the savages didn't have Readers to guide them—and now they do! Just when our only hope is our system of Readers, it's breaking up into factions!//

//So you want to create another one.//

//No. Well, yes—but look, it's the *old* Masters who are tearing the system apart. Surely some of the younger Masters, and almost all the Magisters, would side with us. We could all gather evidence of what Portia and her cronies are doing. Then, if she turns on *us*—//

//You would threaten the Master of Masters?//

//We have to *protect* ourselves!// Tressa insisted. //If we can keep Portia at bay for just a while longer, we'll be safe. She may act like a god, but she's not immortal. She can't live many years longer. If Marina gets her place, our troubles will be over.//

//Tressa, the Council would never choose someone like Marina! Not even to head this Academy—and for Master of Masters they'd choose someone *strong*, especially if at the time the Council is divided. They'd choose someone who could pull—or force—the various factions back into harmony.//

Clearly, Tressa hadn't thought so far. //Still, whoever they choose will have to be more rational than Portia. She's obsessed with the empire's enemies. Either she thinks the savages are causing all our problems—or she *hopes* they are, because that would force everyone to join with her to protect the empire.//

//So Portia is no different from everybody else in blaming the savages.//

//I think she's really convinced. Haven't you noticed in the past few months how Portia suddenly needed to "rest" right after every tremor to shake the city? I overheard her telling Marina—//

//Tressa—you've been eavesdropping on Portia? And you haven't been caught?!//

//Astra, I told you—she's *old*. Both of them are, and their powers are weakening. I Read Portia telling Marina that the tremors are being caused by savage Adepts.//

Such a thought was almost too frightening to contemplate. Tressa took Astra's mental silence as a request for further information. //That tremor yesterday did some damage in The Maze—but a real earthquake would level half the city. If that's the best the Adepts can do, we have nothing to worry about. Portia's fears are the delusion of an old and senile woman.//

//But one still powerful enough to destroy Magisters who conspire against her,// Astra reminded. //Whatever plot *you're* constructing, Tressa, I want no part of it.//

Astra mentally held her breath, afraid to think as the silence between them grew deeper than the void in which they floated. Finally she caught a thought from Tressa: *This one has no love for Portia—she won't betray me.*

Indeed, Astra had no intention of letting this conversation be known—and she let that determination reach Tressa.

But as they were wordlessly parting to return to their bodies, Astra heard another thought: *Someday soon, she'll wish she'd listened to me.*

Although she knew she was meant to "hear" it, Astra made no reply, waiting until Tressa's consciousness had completely departed before she allowed her own turmoil to surface. Were renegade Readers guiding the savage Adepts to destroy the empire? Was that what Master Clement had been doing in The Maze—? Of course they would not try to destroy the city with one or more of their own still within its walls—but had it been a test of their powers?

Surely, oh surely such a plot was possible only in her imagination! If she could talk to someone—but she could trust no one. No one! What was she to do?

Massos charged Zanos at full speed, looking more like a huge black bull than a man as he closed the gap between them. Zanos held his position until the last moment, then made a spinning sidestep, easily evading Massos' outstretched arms and kicking him in the buttocks as he passed.

The blow threw the black gladiator off-stride, nearly propelling him into the wall. He spun and glared at his master, who was calmly backstepping to the center of the wrestling pit, never taking his eyes off his opponent.

Zanos stopped, set himself with legs spread, and beckoned to Massos. "Come on, plow-ox. Even you can do better than that."

The six slave-gladiators in the spectators' seats sucked in a collective breath, but said nothing. For Zanos to challenge Massos to a practice match was one thing—to ridicule him in front of others was to invite injury or death.

Slowly, warily, Massos approached Zanos, circling as he came within arm's length. Zanos followed his opponent only with his eyes, leaving his right side apparently open. Massos made a sudden leap—and was backflipped through the air, landing with a sickening thud.

The big man lay gasping like a fish out of water, and Zanos wondered if he could ever turn all that raw strength into fighting skill. Massos was turning out to be a bad bargain, although his huge size and exotic appearance struck fear into the inexperienced fighters Zanos pitted him against. Sheer strength had won him many matches, but it was getting harder and harder to find appropriate opponents.

The underground chamber remained silent as Zanos knelt to see that there was nothing wrong with Massos except for having the breath knocked out of him. Then Zanos stood up and unsmilingly helped the man back to his feet.

It should *not* have been that easy to defeat him—nor was Massos, of all Zanos' men, capable of deceit in the ring. Indeed, it was one of the problems with his training that he could not learn to feint! But for all Massos' crudeness, even Zanos should not have been able, not only to take him down, but to put him out in only two moves.

He looked up at the other gladiators. "Practice is now over," he announced, watching them glance at one another uneasily. None of them had yet performed.

"Also over is the practice of disobeying my orders," Zanos continued. "When I announce a curfew, there will be no more violations. When I give an order, there will be no backtalk, or the next practice will be with weapons—real, not wooden. Against me."

He wished he could Read which of his men were as out of condition as Massos. They had won their

last games in the arena—although Salamis had barely
defeated his opponent in a match that he should
have had easily, while Aeson was out of the wrestling
season because of a dislocated shoulder and torn
tendons. He had won his match, but possibly at the
cost of his career if that injury did not heal properly.

They had all been slipping, Zanos was sure, because he had counted on their dedication to the
games to keep them on the regimen he had laid out.
Time to tighten the reins.

"I've given all of you privileges that most slaves
only dream of, and you've repaid me with sloppy
performances—and Clavius by losing his life. Now
you will have to *earn* those privileges before you
have them again—and each of you will have to earn
back my trust. Now—five laps around the arena,
today and every day to keep your stamina. Then as
soon as you've cooled off, back to your quarters!"

"Yes, Zanos," came back to him in ragged chorus
as his men hastened to obey. Massos' eyes met his
for a moment, but his defiant look quickly subsided.
Then the black giant hoisted himself out of the pit
and followed the others.

Zanos stayed where he was until they had all gone
but his manservant Ard, who stood watching him
towel off.

Like Zanos, Ard was a Maduran, but about ten
years younger, just past adolescence. While Zanos'
red hair flamed, Ard's was sandy, and his slight build
made it unlikely that he could develop into an athlete. So when Zanos had redeemed his fellow coun-
tryman from the auction block, he had had him
taught to read and write, and put him to work as
chief servant when he bought his villa.

"What are you doing here?" Zanos asked as he
picked up his cloak and slung it over his shoulders.

Ard glanced at the wrestling pit, then at his master. "I know it's not my place to question your
judgment—"

"Then don't," Zanos said tersely. "I know—humiliating Massos in front of the others could turn him against me—but he's not the type to hold a grudge. I showed him he's out of condition. He knows it's from following the other men on their escapades—and if he toes the line, the others will too. He's the strongest, if not the smartest—and he's got a kind of animal wisdom most of us have lost."

His men needed a leader from among themselves—and better the least likely of them to indulge in clever schemes. Clavius had been their leader. Zanos had never questioned his activities because they had become friends. *I can't afford to let that happen again.*

"If we're ever going to get out of the empire," Zanos said to Ard, "we can't afford to lose many more matches. Now, tell me—what are you doing here?"

"You asked to be kept informed of the whereabouts of that female Reader. . . ."

To honor the passing of Master Quantus, all Academy classes had been suspended for the day. Before most of the Readers had left their private meditations, Astra slipped out of the Academy to finish her interrupted journey to Morella's. Bundled up in a gray wool cloak, she walked the streets of The Maze incognito, drawing nothing more than occasional glances.

It was a cold day, threatening rain. The wind through the narrow streets penetrated her cloak, so that by the time she reached her destination she welcomed the wine, roaring fire, and congenial atmosphere of Morella's sitting room.

Morella was in a talkative mood, and Astra maneuvered the conversation around to the subject of gladiators. She told Morella about meeting Zanos at the arena, ending with, "I understand his fighter Clavius was one of your regular customers."

The bordello owner didn't take her cue. Instead, she leaned on the small table between them and studied Astra. Finally she asked, "Just what is it you want to know?"

Astra dropped her eyes in embarrassment. "Was I really that obvious?"

Morella chuckled. "I may not be a Reader, Astra, but in my business we develop an instinct for what someone wants, since he may not know how to ask for it."

Astra nodded. "Discretion is also an important part of your business."

"And yours," the older woman replied. "But there's discretion and discretion. I have no idea what you're searching for, or why—but I trust you. Your judgment gave me back my health. Ask your questions."

"Very well, then." Astra leaned forward eagerly. "Was Clavius a regular customer here?"

"Twice a week, usually. Especially each night before he was scheduled to fight in the bloodgames. He didn't believe the myth about such activities sapping his strength. In fact, he claimed it made him fight that much better."

Astra was puzzled. "Twice a week? How could a slave afford that much . . . entertainment?"

Morella said, "He was a champion, Astra. The stable owners are very generous to their gladiators who bring in prizes and winnings. Such rewards give the gladiators more incentive—Zanos knows that. True, he didn't pay for all of Clavius' visits, but Clea favored him . . . and I, too, must allow some leeway to those who serve me well."

"Does . . . Zanos often come here?"

"Of course he comes in for a drink sometimes, and to tease and talk with my girls. He's a great favorite, but—" She stared at Astra with a puzzled frown. "You didn't know? I'm sorry—you don't live in The Maze, or follow the games, so how would you? It's common knowledge Zanos can't enjoy a woman's favors. In his early arena days, he suffered a sword wound to his vitals. He won the match, but he lost—" Morella shrugged with a sad smile. "And we, too. Such a beautiful man."

Suddenly Astra recalled that Vortius had taunted Zanos about being impotent in their argument at the arena. Why had she forgotten that?

"Morella!"

The cry brought both women to their feet. One of the prostitutes—a dark-skinned girl named Phaeru— met them in the doorway, her eyes wide with fear.

"It's Clea!" she said frantically. "Her door's locked and she won't answer when I knock. Something's wrong!"

Astra followed Morella and Phaeru down the corridor at a brisk pace, opening herself to Reading, no longer concerned about the privacy of possible daytime customers in the nearby rooms. When Morella began pounding on one of the doors, Astra Read past that barrier to the room's interior.

"Morella," she said, putting a restraining hand on the woman's shoulder, "there is no one in that room."

Morella glanced at her. "But it's bolted—"

"The room is empty," Astra said flatly. "She's gone, and so are her belongings. She must have locked the door and left by the window. The shutters are open."

A few minutes later, Phaeru hoisted herself through the open window and into Clea's room. She unbolted the door and admitted Astra and Morella, who told the other girls attracted by the commotion to stay in the corridor.

Astra shivered as she closed the door, cutting off the babble of questions. The room was as cold as the outdoors, the fire of its hearth long dead.

"I don't understand it!" Morella exclaimed as she closed and locked the shutters. "What could have happened? I thought Clea was happy here."

There was no sign of a struggle, but the room held

only its furnishings, no sign of personal possessions. It appeared that Clea had left on her own, but—

Something. A feeling . . . not unlike an odor. Something in the air that Astra's powers could "smell."

A sense of fear. No—deeper than fear.

"Clea left here in a great hurry," the Reader announced, "and in terror."

"Terror?" Morella asked. "Terror of what? Of whom?"

"Her last customer," Astra heard herself say, the wild talent of Reading the past of an object or place taking over her mind. To some degree, she had every talent possible to a Reader, but this one rarely manifested. It felt very strange—as if she were inventing what she said as she spoke, yet did not know what words would come next. "Who was the last person to be with Clea?"

Both Morella and Phaeru frowned, trying to remember.

"I'll have to check my records," the bordello owner said.

"Another thing," Astra continued. "Did Clavius have a favorite? Did he always request Clea?"

Morella stared at her. "Yes . . . every time."

Astra left Morella's feeling perplexed. Each question answered seemed to raise a dozen more. Corruption, she supposed, was to be expected in The Maze, but the mental atmosphere of the brothel was terrifyingly like the feelings she had Read from Tressa. Could there be a connection—?

"Changing professions, Astra?"

She jumped, startled, as Zanos materialized from the alley next to the bordello. "I wish you wouldn't sneak up on me like that!"

"Why, I thought it was impossible to sneak up on a Reader," he said in mock surprise.

Indeed, the only people invisible to a Reader's inner sight were the savage Adepts—when that chilling thought touched her, she focused her powers on him. As before, she could easily Read his surface thoughts and emotions. No, he was not an Adept. Whatever secret he hid, that was not it.

"I—I guess I had my mind on other things," she said as he fell in step beside her. "I was on my way to your villa—but— You were waiting for me, weren't you?" Could the man be an unidentified Reader? It was theoretically possible for someone of very limited powers to slip through the screenings given every child in the empire, developing a minor talent at a later age.

Zanos merely smiled.

"All right—how *did* you know I was in there?"

His smile became a grin. "I told you—I keep informed about everything in The Maze. You were seen going into Morella's, so I decided to escort you back—in case you walk under some more scaffolding," he added placatingly.

So much for special powers. "Very funny," she said, swallowing with difficulty. Talking in the cold air was irritating her throat. *But I've never known a male nonReader to be so friendly with me before.*

Just then the lowering clouds burst, releasing torrents of cold rain. People in the streets ran for shelter.

The Academy was over a mile away.

"Let's go back to Morella's," Astra said, pulling a fold of her cloak over her head.

"No, I have a better idea," Zanos said, putting a guiding arm around her shoulders. "Come with me."

His villa was indeed closer, but by the time they reached it—just as the rain stopped, of course—Astra felt the wet penetrating even her woolen cloak.

Zanos' servants met them at the door. The young woman, Lanna, escorted Astra into a room where a most welcome fire was waiting on the hearth. Brooking no protests, Lanna soon had Astra out of her wet clothes, toweled dry, and wrapped in a warm robe—

but even so, Astra was seized with a fit of sneezing that shook her whole body.

I'm definitely getting my annual cold, Astra thought miserably. Her face was hot, her hands and feet cold, and her throat was getting drier and more painful by the moment.

As if in response to her thought, the manservant, Ard, brought in herb tea. "Zanos will rejoin you shortly, Magister," he announced as he placed the tray before her.

"Thank you," she croaked, wishing she had lemon and honey to mix with the tea. Still, the hot drink soothed her throat as Lanna seated her on soft cushions with her back to the fire and unbraided her hair, combing it out to dry.

The luxurious attention felt strange, but Lanna's touch was unobtrusive, and it was pleasant not to have to fend for herself when she did not feel well.

She looked around the room. It was conservatively decorated in the finest of furnishings and fabrics. Missing something, she realized that in the home of a gladiator she had somehow expected the outrageous—a stuffed leopard, perhaps, or at least a display of weapons on the wall. Instead, a mural that looked recently painted depicted snow-covered mountains on one wall, and the rest were bare.

In the far corner was a low table, holding several musical instruments. A large wooden flute, a five-string harp, a lute . . .

"Does your master play those instruments?" she asked Lanna.

"Yes, Magister. Especially the flute. Many of the street musicians come here for music parties, sharing new songs and having fun with old ones."

Astra felt a twinge of jealousy, for the music curriculum at the Academy left little room for creativity or "fun." Portia preferred that only the classics be taught, discouraging experimentation or improvisation until Astra had enlisted the aid of Master Quantus to persuade her that if no one was allowed to experiment, there would be no works from this generation worthy to become classics.

Sorrow at the reminder of her loss made Astra blink, her sore throat tightening for a moment. She took another sip of tea, and then, to get her mind off the dead musician, she asked Lanna if she might examine the lute.

It was a fine old instrument, but sadly out of tune. Astra carefully tightened the strings, each to its proper pitch, and began to play one of her own compositions. It was contemplative, yet simple—something she often played when she was thinking her way through a problem.

When she finished, she looked up to find Zanos watching from the doorway. This time she knew she hadn't Read him because she had been concentrating on something else—no magic, no mystery.

"Very nice," he said as he entered. He picked up the flute, then joined her by the fire, reclining on a large pillow. "You never mentioned that you are a musician—and a very good one."

"Thank you," she replied, suppressing a cough. "I didn't know *you* played. Lanna tells me you hold music parties."

"Yes—the professionals put up with my playing," he said wryly. "As a boy I spent much more time practicing swordsmanship than music, and now that I have time for music I'm too old to develop great skill."

Lanna put the pins back into Astra's rebraided hair, and quietly left the room. Alone with Zanos, Astra found herself once again examining her feelings about him. *Why should I feel uneasy?* she asked herself. *He seems to want to be my friend. Surely I could Read any ulterior motive.* But part of the tension she felt was coming from Zanos, she realized. He was smiling at her as she tunelessly strummed the lute, but a part of his mind was studying her with great curiosity.

Would it be wise to tell him what she'd discovered at Morella's?

Suddenly he put the flute to his lips and began playing a tune she found vaguely familiar. Without thinking, she began to harmonize on the lute. The tension faded as their musical talents merged into a single entity. On the second go-round, the song took on a vitality of its own, bringing Astra a joy she had never known before. Zanos was wrong to deprecate his talent—he had a natural vigor, a perfect sense of rhythm, and an inventive style.

Astra's spirit soared with the music's intensity, and she Read outward almost without being aware of it. Her powers focused on Ard and Lanna, who were in the hall outside—dancing to the music! Her smile broadened as she "watched" them and felt their shared pleasure. The movements were a romance for them, expressing love for each other—

Other minds intruded. Male Readers!

Astra abruptly stopped playing, causing Zanos to do the same. Her throat tightened painfully as she said, "You're about to have two more guests." She jumped to her feet. "Two male Readers. Magisters. Zanos, we mustn't see each other—in fact, I'd rather they didn't know I was here."

"I understand," he said, now also on his feet. "Go into the kitchen."

Suppressing a coughing fit, Astra merely nodded as she put down the lute and quickly left the room. She shielded her mind as best she could. All she could do now was hope that the two Magisters wouldn't bother to scan the villa.

Their names were Darien and Primus. Their voices carried from the entry hall to the kitchen just loudly enough for Astra to overhear without Reading. Zanos did not invite them into the comfortable music room, she noted.

"We know you must be looking forward to the wrestling season, Zanos," Darien was saying. "It will give you a chance to recover from your losses in the gladiatorial games."

"And what does that have to do with you Readers?" Zanos asked, although his tone of voice suggested he already knew.

"We're here to protect you from further losses," Primus said glibly. "You want to be certain all your wrestlers are healthy and fit to compete. Magister Darien and I have the duty of Reading the health of the wrestlers this season."

So, Astra realized, *another part of the corruption puzzle: extortion.*

"And just how much would it cost to make sure my wrestlers are judged healthy?" Zanos asked quietly.

"Merely ten marks of gold," Darien replied.

"For each of us," Primus added.

Zanos laughed—a loud, hearty laugh that astonished both men. "I hear that when one of you Readers gets injured, any other Readers near you suffer the pain," he said. "Is that right? Good—then I only have to beat one of you, for both of you to fully understand my answer—"

Astra Read Zanos' hand grab Primus' throat, hard enough to terrify him. The gladiator shoved the Reader toward the door. Darien got there first, opened the door, and fled into the street. Zanos pushed Primus through the open doorway and watched in satisfaction as the Reader fell on the wet cobbles, then scrambled to his feet, following his colleague.

"You'll pay for this indignity, Zanos!" Primus screamed as he backed away from the villa, shaking his fist. "You'll pay dearly!"

The gladiator didn't reply, just closed the door. But as he bolted it and reentered the music room, Astra Read anger mixed with fear. She rejoined him, noting how grim he looked.

"I knew they'd be coming sooner or later," he told her. "Lakus, my former owner, told me last year that the Readers wait until a stable owner has tasted prosperity—and wants to keep it—before they start demanding money."

Astra blinked. "Did you think I was—?"

"Involved in that? No," he replied, "or you wouldn't be trying to help me. You did say earlier that you were coming to tell me something you discovered at Morella's. What was it?"

"I think I found out how Clavius was given the white lotus," she told him. "Clea, one of Morella's girls, was Clavius' favorite. And now she's disappeared. Her last customer was someone called Varan—"

Zanos shook his head. "You're on the wrong trail," he said firmly. "Varan is a harmless old man who drinks too much. No one could trust him to be sober enough to do his part in a conspiracy. Clea probably got a message after Varan left. I understand what you're thinking—Clea was paid to give Clavius white lotus in his wine whenever he visited her . . . until that last time before his final match."

"Yes," Astra nodded, coughing. "The exertion of combat used up the last of the drug in his bloodstream. Then his body failed him at the critical moment, and Metrius was able to kill him."

"I don't believe in coincidences," Zanos said. "Clavius' death, Clea's disappearance, two Readers coming here today—all of it is part of the same plot . . . a plot too big for me to fight."

"Too big for you to fight *alone*," Astra corrected. "You need help from others."

He looked at her, puzzled. "What others? Vortius and his friends have half the city in their grip."

"Others who have as much to lose as you do: the stable owners. If they've been paying corrupt Readers not to disqualify their fighters, then each owner must be as angry as you are. If *all* of you refuse to pay, the extortionists would have to back down or there would be no wrestling matches this season. That would deprive some very important, powerful people—including the Emperor—of their entertainment."

Zanos sat there for a long moment, considering her words. Astra realized that his reluctance to jump at the idea came from the concept of having to unite with his rivals. In his world, each man fought alone for survival.

But finally he nodded. "It might work, Astra. Thank you. I hope I can convince Lakus, Gareth, and the others to cooperate."

"You can do it," she said with a smile—and was again seized with a sneezing fit.

"You're sick!" Zanos said. "Let me have Lanna prepare a room for you—"

"No!" she insisted. "I must go back to the Academy. It's nothing but a cold, Zanos—just an annoyance that will be gone in a few days. If my clothes are dry—"

He did not argue, but walked her back to the Academy. It was a long and miserable walk for Astra, trying to respond to the stories Zanos told, to hide from him just how bad she was feeling. Fever was making her dizzy by the time she stumbled into the infirmary—but the healer on duty was busy with three little girls and left Astra to brew her own tea with lemon and honey to take back to her room.

When she woke the next morning she felt even worse, but told herself that if she just moved around—

She skipped breakfast, drank more tea, and went to teach her first lesson in a fog of pain. What voice she had was an octave lower than usual, and the strain of scolding a student who hadn't done her practice sent her into a coughing fit that tinged her handkerchief with blood. The child fled, and moments later Master Claudia came into the music room. "Astra! How could you let yourself get into this condition?"

"Really," Astra tried to protest, the words clogging her swollen throat, "it's nothing. Just a cold—"

"Cold!" Claudia exclaimed. "Can't you Read for yourself how swollen your tonsils are? Child, you have a septic throat—you must be delirious with fever not to realize how serious it is—and if we don't get you isolated, half the Academy could be down with it. Astra—are you trying to kill us all?"

Chapter Three

Red.

The whole world was fiery red. Astra stumbled through heat and pain, seeking the coolness of winter. She fell to her hands and knees in a narrow lane—Zanos appeared and helped her to her feet. They clung to each other as the ground shook even more violently than it had the day they met. An eerie laugh, louder than the earthquake's rumble, caused her to look toward the mouth of the alley—to see the sorcerer Lenardo laughing at their terror.

He raised his hands. Sunfire lit him from behind, throwing his face into shadow as he flung lightning at Astra and Zanos.

The gladiator put out his hand and warded off the attack, turning the blazing missiles to harmless rainbows, lighting the face of the sorcerer in lurid tones.

It was no longer Lenardo, but Vortius! In the midst of the dream, the transformation seemed to hold great significance, but as the colors faded, so did Astra's conviction.

She was lying in a hospital bed, so weak that she could hardly Read at all. Concerned faces of healers floated in and out of her range of vision, blurred and wavering. She struggled for breath, her throat raw, her chest aching as she fought for air.

Finally, Master Portia stood at the foot of her bed,

dressed all in white, carrying a baby wrapped in cloth of gold, but pale and deathly still.

"I'm sorry," Portia said coldly.

"My baby!" Astra cried. "Please! Please let me have my child!"

"The baby is dead," Portia told her.

Tears came to Astra's eyes. "No! It can't be!"

"If you refuse to believe me," Portia said, "Read for yourself."

With great effort, Astra focused her powers—

The baby wailed.

The sound grew, encompassing the world, a universe of golden light, realm of the Sun God. He reached down to touch Astra's chest, letting cool fire flow into her. Gentle, cooling darkness lovingly embraced her, carrying her away from pain to a place of welcome rest. . . .

Astra woke in a strange bed, still very weak, but nonetheless feeling *good*. The pain was gone from her chest and throat, and her mind felt clear. She was in a small, dimly lit infirmary room. To her right, an apprentice healer was asleep in a chair. Astra Read outward, and found that she could Read a considerable distance, although nowhere near her usual range.

The young healer awoke with a start, and barely managed to suppress a gasp of surprise. "You're awake!" she cried, jumping to her feet. "Oh, thank the gods! You were so close to death, first with fever and pneumonia, and then the coma—"

"How long have I been here?" Astra demanded. It couldn't have been more than a day or two.

"Three weeks!" the young healer said.

Even after Master Claudia confirmed it, Astra found it difficult to believe she had lost that much time from her life. Her septic throat had spread infection to her lungs and brought her to death's door, the healers told her—and then, two days ago, she had gone into a coma, and they had feared brain fever.

But the infection had cleared, the fever had gone, and—

"We've never seen anything like this," one of the healers told her. "We find no trace of infection, but you should rest here for a few days to build back your strength."

In her weakened state, Astra was in no mood to argue. Her first priority was food, and she astonished the healers by gulping down the gruel they brought and demanding something more satisfying. She had never been so hungry in her life!

Then she lay back and remembered her strange fever dreams. They were no longer clear in her mind, but a few images still haunted her. She fell asleep before she could try to make sense of them.

The following day, her strength returning, Astra was allowed to have visitors. The first one was Tressa.

"Enjoying your vacation, Astra?" she asked glibly as she entered, then dropped her false smile as soon as the door was closed. "Don't Read!" she whispered sharply. "They're supposed to grant privacy to recovering patients, so it should be safe to talk for a short time."

"Talk about what?" Astra demanded, her apprehension aroused as always by Tressa's conspiratorial attitude. "What has happened now?"

"I didn't think they'd tell you, but you must know: another Master died two days ago—Master Julius, the head of the hospital in Termoli. Portia had him retested—and *failed*!"

Astra stared at her. "But he was a healer for longer than I've been in this world!"

"I know," Tressa nodded sagely, "but that didn't save him from Portia's wrath. He was supposed to be married off to blunt his powers—but he chose to take poison instead."

Astra looked away, fighting to keep her Reading from manifesting and giving away her upset to other nearby Readers.

Tressa touched her arm. "*Now* will you listen to me?" she all but pleaded. "We need each other—"

"To do what?" Astra snapped. "Start civil war among the Readers? Use extortion against the Masters? Where will it end, Tressa? In the destruction of the whole Reader system?"

Tressa drew back—even without Reading, Astra could see astonishment and anger fighting in her face. And Astra understood why: Tressa was right that something had to be done—yet how could a pair of Magister Readers kept strictly under Portia's thumb do anything but destroy themselves if they attempted to expose the Master of Masters?

Before she could point that out, Tressa stood, and left without another word.

Astra fought down tears of frustration—and dread. What *was* the right thing to do? Master Julius had obviously seen no way to fight Portia—or else he had tried and failed. But Tressa was right that Portia couldn't live forever; perhaps the young Readers could just pretend to notice nothing, and wait it out until eventually Portia was gone. And if her successor was equally corrupt? Well, they could deal with that when and if it happened.

Astra didn't believe it could happen. The Academy system was set up so that Readers could not be corrupted by power. All their needs were cared for, but they were not allowed to own property or hold office. Portia was an anomaly. Perhaps she had bribed or threatened some Readers, like Darien and Primus—or perhaps she had just allowed people like Vortius to do so?

What *was* Portia's connection with Vortius?

The next day brought solitude and boredom to the rapidly recovering patient, and she decided to test her powers. Carefully positioning her body on the bed, she left it, reveling in the feeling of freedom. She drifted through the infirmary to the maternity rooms.

Many women of Tiberium came to the Readers for care during pregnancy; usually one of the midwives went to a woman's home when she gave birth, but if it was judged that the birth would be difficult, the woman was admitted a few days before her child was due.

Thus there was only one patient in the maternity section. Astra was about to "move" on past without prying, according to the rules granting privacy to patients, when the young woman's grief reached out to her errant powers, capturing her attention against her will.

The woman had lost her child. She lay tensely on the bed, her mind futilely circling in grief. Astra was forcefully reminded of her fever dream—

So that's where it came from!

She dragged her attention away from the sorrowing woman, mortified. Readers were trained as children not to Read while they slept. Astra's training had taken much longer than that of the other girls; her powers had refused to rest at night despite months on end of being jolted harshly awake by a monitoring Reader each time her mind reached outward in her sleep.

To avoid Reading the patient, Astra concentrated on the room, recognizing it from her dream. But the rest . . . Portia visiting a nonReader? Conducting the funeral for the innocent herself, dressed all in white? And the dead baby wrapped in cloth of gold? Surely not for this grieving woman's benefit.

Portia wasn't a healer—Astra had never known her to touch an ill or injured person, even in an emergency. Of course she would have had medical training years ago, but the Master of Masters was never involved with such things now.

Astra's dream, then, could not have been mere Reading of this poor woman's loss. Her grief had triggered something—a memory, something connected with the infirmary . . . a time when Portia *had* come here to inform a new mother—

My mother! Astra realized in utter astonishment. With the total conviction of her wild powers Reading the history of that room in the maternity ward, she *knew* she had Read her own mother's memories!

Astra had learned her mother's story in gossip and random thought. Since young Readers were always separated from their families when their powers were discovered, she had been no different from the other girls at first—except that she had lived here at the Academy since she could remember, while others were brought here at six, seven, or eight.

But the adult Readers knew the scandal, and inevitably it leaked to the young girls in training—and under the harsh disciplines of Readers' training they grasped at something to gossip about. No adult had ever told Astra her parents' story; the pretense, even today, was that she should never know it. As if that would help her ward off the suspicions always flung her way!

Eventually she had pieced together the whole story.

Twenty-five years ago, the city of Zendi had been inside the empire's northern border. The savages, after a long and bloody battle, had succeeded in pushing the border all the way south to Adigia. Thousands of refugees overflowed the small town of Adigia, many of them wounded in the fighting. Among the injured were some male Readers from the Zendi Academy who had escaped being killed by the enemy. Healers from the central cities, especially Tiberium, had rushed to Adigia to deal with the many sick and wounded.

The rule regarding male and female Readers not meeting had been suspended for healers in the emergency. Thus it was possible for Master Anthony, a swordsman and musician, to become the patient of Master Cassandra of the Tiberium Academy.

Not long after his recovery, and before her recall

to Tiberium, something . . . happened between the two Masters. Love? Perhaps. Certainly there was no way for Cassandra to hide the fact that she had violated her Reader's Oath of celibacy.

Apparently she had been kept a virtual prisoner in the Academy until her child was born. Not long afterward, she somehow managed to escape from the Academy, from the empire entirely, never to be heard of again.

Leaving me, the symbol of her shame, as a ward of the state. How she must have hated me, not to have taken me with her.

Two healers entered the infirmary room. One of them, Master Claudia, said to the distraught young woman, "We know how you are grieving, Celia, but you must understand that the baby's stillbirth was in no way your fault." The other Master handed the woman a cup of wine, which Astra could Read contained a sedative.

As the patient drank, Claudia spoke soft, hypnotic words. The woman slowly relaxed, her mind entering a trancelike state. The two healers' minds gently touched hers, deepening the trance, then delicately worked to lessen her grief in ways that Astra only partially understood.

They were using techniques of advanced medical training. Astra had received basic training in such techniques at Gaeta, but these were methods she would have learned only if she had become a healer rather than a music teacher. In her time as a student at the Gaeta hospital—

TERROR! PAIN!

Dozens of Readers' agony screamed at Astra, buffeting her like a small craft in an ocean storm. She could not shut her mind against the flood of fear and PAIN!

//Help!// she screamed mentally, helpless in her out-of-body state to close her mind to the inundation.

Master Claudia looked up, her concentration broken. //Help me!// Astra pleaded.

"Stay here!" Claudia commanded her assistant as she hurried out of the room. Astra fought to reorient herself. She had to get back to her body, shut herself away from this pain, but hundreds of emotions kept tearing at her—

//Astra!//

Master Claudia's mental voice was like a hand firmly grasping her by the wrist, pulling her back to the physical world . . . and indeed, the healer was holding her wrist as she reentered her body, feeling as though she'd fallen from a great height.

Master Claudia stood, breathing a sigh of relief. "Thank the gods! Astra, what were you doing out of body when you're still so weak—?"

"Gaeta!" Astra gasped, now able to make sense of what she had experienced. "Something terrible's happened at Gaeta!"

"The seacoast town?" Zanos frowned. He didn't understand what Astra was so upset about. "What about it?"

Astra swallowed hard. "Late last night, an earthquake devastated the hospital there. Many patients and healers were injured—and some were killed, including five Readers."

"Friends of yours?" He had come here expecting to find her feeling better, not in the midst of a personal tragedy.

"Acquaintances, some of them. But it was enough that they were Readers. I felt it happen," she added, and suddenly he understood. In her world, no one dwelt in isolation—and he felt a strange pang for the threats he had made to Darien and Primus.

But Astra was continuing, "Zanos, it's more than just the deaths of Readers—in a natural disaster, such things happen. But this wasn't natural—they were *murdered*."

"What?" He could see that she believed it—and with a Reader's powers, perhaps she had good cause.

"That earthquake was no act of the gods," Astra explained. "Master Portia used her powers to search the territory immediately afterward. She witnessed two spies from the savage lands, sneaking back over the border—a powerful Adept and a renegade Reader."

This was indeed frightening news—and no rumor of it had penetrated The Maze. "She's sure the two savages had something to do with the earthquake?" Zanos asked.

"Why, they bragged about it! When Portia confronted him, mind to mind, the Reader declared there was nothing the savages couldn't do, combining Reading and Adept powers. Portia alerted the border guards, but the spies escaped."

Although Zanos found nothing magical about evading the border guards, the rest of the story— "Just *one* Adept guided by a Reader—setting off an earthquake? Surely they can't have such strength!"

"Master Portia found no other savages, and I'm told she did a lot of searching. The Emperor called for a special closed meeting of the senate, where she made a full report. They're probably still debating what to do, though there's little doubt that when the citizens hear about Gaeta there'll be a public outcry for war. The savages can't be allowed to get any bolder, any more powerful."

As soon as the senate session is over, the news will be all over The Maze, Zanos thought. "How much more powerful can they become?" he wondered aloud—and Astra gave him an unexpected answer.

"I'm afraid to imagine. They've already learned how to bring the dead back to life."

At his shocked stare, Astra nodded emphatically. "It's true. The renegade Reader was a boy named Torio, who was killed last year trying to defect to the savages. A border guard put an arrow through his heart, but the other renegade Reader—Lenardo the

Traitor—carried the body back to his friends, where they resurrected Torio and made him one of them. Now he's helping the savages!"

"And your Council of Masters thinks this attack was a preparation for a full-scale invasion of the empire?"

"Obviously—Zanos, they've been pushing back the borders for years, but now they're directly attacking Readers. First the Adigia Academy, now Gaeta—I can't believe even the savages would deliberately attack a hospital, except that it contained as large a concentration of Readers as any Academy. They're trying to wipe out our system of Masters and Magisters, for they've proved that the failed Readers on the Path of the Dark Moon are no match for their savage arts."

Zanos noticed the high color in Astra's cheeks, her paleness otherwise, and attempted to soothe her. "I'm sorry. I didn't mean to upset you—"

"It's not *you*," she replied. "It's the savages. What are we going to do?"

"That's up to the Emperor and the senate. In the meantime," he added, deliberately changing the subject, "I want to thank you. I took your advice about the stable owners. It took a full night of arguing and coaxing, but they finally agreed—not one of us paid those Readers this month. And it's working! So far, all the stables have been represented at the matches, their best wrestlers performing."

"Congratulations," she said. "I'm glad the idea worked. There's been no retaliation from Vortius and his friends?"

"Not even threats. No one has seen Vortius lately. He's not at his town house or his villa in the southlands. So far as anyone knows, he's left the empire."

"But where would he go?" she asked in amazement.

Zanos smiled at her sheltered innocence. "Surely you know both trade and smuggling go on outside the empire. I'm sure Vortius will be back—but if it takes a while, and he makes a rich haul, it may not be worth his while to try to break the united strength of the gladiators on his return." *And maybe before he tries it, I will be far away from here.*

"When will you be out of the infirmary?" he asked, looking around the tiny room. "I'd like to celebrate our success with a music party, and you're the first person I'm inviting."

"I'll be out in another day or so, and I'd love to come," she said eagerly, then frowned. "But your friends would be uneasy with a Reader in their midst."

"Well, we won't tell them." He shrugged. "My servants won't say anything. Just don't wear your robes or give your title. Play your lute with us. Once everyone gets to know you, you being a Reader won't matter."

"And if they ask where I come from? What I do?"

"They won't," Zanos replied. "Not in The Maze."

"Very well, then, I'll be there." And she smiled, that beautiful smile he'd waited so long to see again.

Zanos left the Academy less lighthearted than when he'd entered. Surely Astra's news about Gaeta and the savages would mean war. But he wasn't as concerned about war with the savages as about a widespread search for spies in Tiberium.

How ironic . . . I'm finally free of Vortius and his kind, only to be endangered by Adepts from the savage lands. But if I had the powers they're reported to have . . .

The next day war was officially proclaimed, although there was no mention in the public statements of Adepts having caused the earthquake that had nearly destroyed the Gaeta hospital. Zanos sidestepped the sudden fervor for the war effort and concentrated on readying his wrestlers for the next evening's matches. He went to bed satisfied that each of his men was ready.

Sometime after midnight, Ard awakened him to give him a note.

Zanos read it, dressed, strapped on his sword, and almost forgot to grab up his cloak as he ran out the front door.

Minutes later, he entered the Temple of Hesta. Serafon led him to one of the anterooms.

Massos lay on a large table, more dead than alive. He was covered with cuts and bruises, and the gladiator didn't have to touch him to know that many of his bones were broken.

Zanos swore mightily as he strove to hold his anger in check. In the back of his mind rang the sound of Vortius' mocking laughter.

"Who did this?" he demanded finally.

"Cutter. That was all he could tell me. He didn't know *why*."

"*I* know why," Zanos growled. "This is Vortius' way of telling me he's back, and knows I'm the one who stopped his extortion. Cutter must have been waiting to see which of my men would break training. I thought that for a while at least—"

He left the sentence unfinished, not really angry at his fighter. He had misread Massos, humiliated him in front of his teammates, and really believed he wouldn't retaliate with an act of disobedience. *He's paying for my mistake.*

"Zanos." Serafon's tone was quiet but sharp. "What are you going to do?"

"Answer Vortius' message," he said curtly. "For the moment—just for the moment—I'll still leave Vortius to you. But Cutter is mine."

Cutter and his gang were well paid to act for those too fastidious to fight their own battles. Everyone in The Maze knew where they celebrated after one of their dirty jobs. And at this late hour—

"Can you take care of him yourself?" Zanos asked, nodding at Massos.

The old woman sighed. "Yes. He will be all right . . . eventually."

"Fine," he said as he stripped off sword and scabbard. Unlike Cutter, Zanos had to remain within the law to continue in his profession. Even in The Maze, Aventine law would not protect him if he used a weapon.

Besides, he wouldn't need it.

The Crying Maiden tavern was a dimly-lit meeting place for thugs and cutpurses. On this night there were few patrons—except for the six men Zanos was looking for. They sat at a large circular table by the far wall, none with his back to the room's center. Their rowdiness had emptied the tables all around them, Zanos noted. So much the better.

"Massos is going to live!" he announced from the doorway, and smiled as the six stopped talking and looked in his direction. He entered with exaggerated calm, spotted the innkeeper, and tossed him a small pouch of coins.

Behind the gladiator and to his left, two stools scraped away from a table and two men left quietly, closely followed by the innkeeper. Several other patrons kept their seats, watching and waiting.

The six denizens of the gutter stared at Zanos with eyes full of contempt and strong wine.

"You recognize me," he said. "That's good. You're not too drunk to understand. I'm going to assume that you're smart enough not to get up when you fall down. Because if you get up, you will die."

Cutter, who was sitting directly across from him, let out a derisive laugh, revealing rotted and missing teeth. "Why don't you just go home, Zanos? You're not in the arena now. And you can't count, eunuch."

The insult drew laughs from the others. Zanos hadn't known his deception had reached this deeply into the Maze. "Oh, I can count, all right. In fact, I can do a lot of things that would surprise you. . . ." He noticed all of them slowly dropping their hands below the table, shoulder muscles tensing.

He braced himself. "I'm here because I got the

message you brought me from Vortius. And now you're going to deliver my answer back to—"

"NOW!"

Sure enough, the table flipped over at Zanos, wine jugs and tankards flying. He easily jumped out of the way as they staggeringly launched themselves at him.

His jump back became a spinning kick, connecting with the attacker on the far left and breaking ribs. The man fell back, screaming, and collided with the thug beside him, taking both of them down.

The other four moved in two directions, seeking to trap the gladiator in a circle. Zanos' left hand snaked out and grabbed up a chair by the edge of its seat. He turned and threw it to his right with lightning speed, nearly taking off the head of that thug, leaving him unconscious.

Now a triangle opposed him, all three in his range of vision, Cutter directly in front of him. The dark-haired leader yelled something at the one on Zanos' right, but the ploy didn't fool him; he looked to his left and ducked as a wine jug sailed past his ear and smashed against the wall.

The one who had been knocked over by Broken Ribs was on his feet again, charging from between Cutter and the jug thrower. He came in low, arms spread for a tackle.

Zanos set himself and carefully timed a knee-kick to the man's chin. The head snapped loudly back, and it was a corpse that knocked him into a small table and sent him sprawling, the hem of his cloak wrapping around his legs.

Seeing their chance, Cutter and the other two leaped. Zanos unhooked the clasp of his cloak, then rolled out of the garment just as the first one was on him.

Zanos' legs snapped up, both feet catching the thug in his groin and using the momentum to carry him over the gladiator's head. He crashed into the wall, slid down it, and did not get up.

Cutter and his last henchman came at the fighter from two directions, murder in their eyes. The henchman reached him first, aiming a kick at Zanos' head. The gladiator twisted out of the way, and the attacker lost his balance, fell backwards, and hit his head on a stone pillar.

Zanos twisted the other way, but Cutter's kick grazed his left temple. Ignoring the pain behind his eyes, he kept rolling until he was on his back again and could grasp the leg of a chair. He tossed it at Cutter's knees. Wood and bone collided, and the man roared in pain as he staggered backwards.

Zanos got to his feet. The two of them faced off across the room, neither moving for a long moment. Then Cutter's right hand slapped his hip and came up with his throwing knife by the blade. One of the corner spectators yelled a warning as Cutter let the blade fly.

But the gladiator didn't move. The missile missed its target, and Zanos deftly plucked it from the air by its hilt.

Cutter staggered backwards again, this time in shock, and someone muttered an oath. Cutter's blade *never* missed.

Zanos smiled nastily as he flipped the weapon into the air and caught it by the tip.

Cutter's eyes darted left and right, but there was no one to help him.

He jumped to his left, grabbed up a small table as a shield—and let out a small gurgle as he fell over, the hilt of his own knife sticking out of his throat.

Corpse and table hit the floor with a loud crash, and then the room was silent. No applause, no cheers for the champion. The only roaring was in Zanos' ears. He fought dizziness as he bent for his cloak. The throb of bruises pushed through his mental barriers, and pain in his right knee caused him to limp as he left the tavern.

This is insane, he thought bitterly. *I'll have to kill*

half the city before summer! There must be a better way of getting the money I need. We have to be out of the empire before we're caught in the war.

"We" now included Astra. With the savages intent on murdering Readers, she was in grave danger. And if the savages had such powers as Zanos had heard, his band of refugees would need a Reader to guide them.

How he would persuade her, he didn't know—but the time to approach her would be when he was finally ready to go. In the meantime, he must try to prevent her Reading his plans, such as they were.

Suddenly he stopped walking. A new plan came to him, full-blown. He laughed at its simplicity. *Astra is right. I can't defeat my enemies alone, so I'll get myself an ally—a very powerful ally!*

The next morning, he dressed in his most impressive clothes, went to the royal palace, and requested an audience with the Emperor. Zanos usually shunned his celebrity status, but this day he exploited it, adding all the charm and wit he could muster to work his way through the Emperor's retainers.

Eventually he was escorted to one of the conference chambers, and left to wait for the Emperor. The portly, middle-aged man greeted him warmly, clasping the gladiator's upper arms as though the two men were comrades in arms.

"Ah, the arena games just haven't been the same since you retired, Zanos," the ruler said.

"Thank you, majesty," Zanos smiled.

"You've come to make a contribution to the war effort?"

"Yes," Zanos nodded. "As the war fleet's launching date approaches, each citizen must do his part to raise funds. I'm offering as my contribution a special arena match—myself against any single opponent of your choosing—with admission receipts to be donated to the military."

"Excellent!" said the Emperor. "I like that! The

greatest gladiator of the century coming out of retirement. Why, every citizen in the empire would pay to see that—except the Readers, of course," he added with a laugh.

Zanos hid his annoyance with a tight smile. He had no love for this soft, self-indulgent aristocrat sending thousands of people to war while he stayed safely at home.

"But finding an opponent worthy of you," the ruler was continuing, "someone who can truly test your mettle . . . I thank you for bringing me this delightful challenge. I will send out word, and when such an opponent is found, the match will be announced."

Zanos left the palace, inwardly smug. Now that the Emperor himself had an interest in Zanos' affairs, the criminals would have to back off. Even better, this match would generate heavy gambling. If he wagered everything he owned on the outcome, Zanos could win enough money to make his dream a reality.

Just a little while longer, and I'll be going home . . . home!

In the days of preparation for war, the city of Tiberium began to change. Political and social factions which ordinarily ignored or antagonized each other united against the threat of the savages. The Emperor and the senate met daily, as did the Council of Masters.

Astra was released from the infirmary into an Academy whose daily routine was interrupted by senators and generals seeking audience with Portia at all hours.

She picked up the threads of her duties, but with a keener interest in both state and Academy politics. She used her powers carefully, not deliberately spying, but attempting to separate the strange facts from the even stranger rumors. Slowly she gained a picture of a nervous senate wanting to protect Aventine citizens from further attacks by the savages—but also

hoping that the army could regain the lands lost to
the Adepts in the past few decades.

"It could happen," Zanos agreed when she told
him her speculations. She had stolen an hour from
errands Portia had assigned her, and found him willing to take a break from his strenuous training for the
upcoming bout. Nothing she told him violated her
Reader's Oath—and she quickly found that the rumors in the Academies were equally current in The
Maze.

Despite the chill air, Zanos shone with sweat in
the winter sunshine. He had been practicing with a
wooden sword against some complex piece of ma-
chinery which, Astra noted, swung around to strike
the athlete whose blow landed off the target. As she
stood next to him, she became aware of the salt smell
of his fresh sweat, and realized that he was wearing
almost nothing—just a sort of breechclout.

His muscles rippled, even when he merely bent to
pick up a rough towel to wipe himself off after his
exertion, and Astra noticed once again how huge and
powerful he was. She remembered him holding the
collapsing building off the children they had rescued
the day they met . . . his strength inspired her trust
somehow, as if he could protect her. But that was
nonsense—no mere man's strength meant anything
against the powers of the savage Adepts.

Zanos tossed the towel over the apparatus, and
pulled a woolen tunic over his head. Not noticing
Astra's blush, he continued, "Ships are massing in
the harbors. The army will probably attack the western coast, then march inland. If they move fast
enough, they might take a good piece of territory
before the Adepts unite against them. But when that
happens, there is going to be a slaughter."

"It's the Adepts who will do the slaughtering,"
Astra said, letting Zanos lead her away from the
practice field in the direction of his home. "I've
heard that the sorcerers can turn ships to stone. If
that's true, our troops may never reach the land!"

"Every battle, every war has its ifs," Zanos pointed out. "A gladiator faces them every time he steps into the arena: he might lose his life if his opponent is the stronger, or the smarter—or he might die simply because the gods frown on him that day."

"Yes," said Astra, as Zanos opened the door to his house and led her into the music room. "That brings me to the real reason I'm here. Why are you going to fight in the arena again?"

He explained that it was his contribution to the war effort, told her of the Emperor's excitement—but she was not satisfied.

"Why would you want to endanger your life again? Surely not just out of patriotism."

Zanos gave her a strange smile, and an old feeling came back to her—the sense that he was hiding something very important from her. A part of her wanted to violate the Reader's Code and purposely invade his thoughts, but she wouldn't, couldn't do it even if she suspected him to be an enemy of the state. This man stirred up emotions in her that she could neither deny nor fully comprehend.

"Vortius is back in Tiberium," he said finally. "I plan to use the match to keep him from attacking me. I didn't tell you I was back in training because I knew you wouldn't come anywhere near the arena unless you had to—like the day we met. I knew you'd hear about it anyway."

"I may not come to watch you fight," Astra said quietly, "but I care what happens to you—as a friend. Is this why you never held your music party?"

"I've spent all my time getting back in training. My opponent has been chosen and is being brought to Tiberium. The Emperor will set the date for the contest in the next few days. It will probably be just before the first day of spring. So I've had no time for music. Besides, you know what a terrible player I am."

"I know no such thing," Astra said as she got up to

retrieve the two musical instruments from the corner. Zanos was still protesting as she handed him his flute, then sat down again to tune her instrument. With a smile, she challenged him with an intriguing tune that she made up on the spot. Zanos raised his instrument and chased musically after her, harmonizing as Astra repeated the main theme.

The joy she experienced that day was deepened in the following weeks. Any evening Astra had free from her duties, she knew she would find Zanos at home—his strict physical regimen meant no carousing, and an early bedtime.

So they shared private music parties, giving her brief respite from the increased apprehension in the Reader system. The split in the Council of Masters seemed to be getting worse. More students, Magisters, and Masters were sent to walk the Path of the Dark Moon. Astra held her tongue, tried to hold her wild powers in check, and kept out of Portia's way except when sent for. She didn't have to work at avoiding Tressa; the other young Magister stayed well out of Astra's environment.

The day of the benefit in the gladiatorial arena was announced. Zanos' match against his mysterious opponent would be the main event of the day. Two days before, Astra visited him, hoping it would not be for the last time.

"Don't worry," he told her with a smile. "I'll win. I know what I'm doing, Astra."

"All the same, I've heard about this Mallen," Astra said. "He's traveled all around the empire, taking any combat challenge. He's *undefeated*."

"So am I," he reminded her, "and I've got much more experience than he has. Don't worry about me. Tell you what—as soon as the victory parties are over, we'll have that music party I promised you. You'll like my musician friends, I think."

But Astra couldn't turn to another subject. She found it hard to look at him as she said, "Would it offend you if I told you I pray every day for your victory?"

"No," he said gently, "and I thank you for it. I know you won't be watching or Reading the match, but keep your ears open that day—my victory cry will be louder than the applause of the entire stadium!"

Astra tried to smile encouragement, despite her apprehension. *Two days . . . I wonder what I'll be doing then—besides worrying about you?*

"In two days," Portia informed her, "you will be the bride's attendant at a wedding—Tressa's."

Astra, already startled at finding the Master of Masters waiting up for her, went numb with shock.

When she did not answer, Portia continued, "For some time now, I have had grave doubts about Tressa's competency as a Reader. After investigating, we have decided that she is not truly skilled enough for the upper ranks; those who tested her for Magister must have been mistaken. It can happen that several Masters are not at their best on one particular day. After all, even Readers are only human."

Astra knew, almost without thinking it, that her assignment as Tressa's attendant was another punishment duty—or perhaps a warning. She wasn't Tressa's friend; like Astra, Tressa had no real friends at the Academy. On the other hand, it was possible that Portia had chosen Astra for this task because she truly was the person who knew Tressa best.

"As you wish, Master Portia," Astra said carefully. "Has Tressa been informed?"

"About an hour ago. I have been waiting for you since. You have spent much time outside the Academy recently, Astra. Please advise me of such excursions in the future—with the impending war, it is necessary that I be able to contact all my Readers at a moment's notice."

"Yes, Master Portia," replied Astra with all the humility she could muster. Her heart was pounding, and it took all her control not to broadcast her anxiety.

Portia dismissed her, and Astra fled down the corridor and across the courtyard to the dormitory, letting her Reading open wide.

Tressa was sitting on the side of her bed, closed to Reading. Astra knocked at her door, then opened it without waiting for a reply. Lamplight glittered off the blade of the knife in Tressa's hand. She stared at it with rapt attention, as though the weapon were a holy object.

"You know?" Tressa asked flatly.

"Portia told me," Astra said, trying to catch her breath, not knowing what to say.

The fierceness was gone from Tressa's eyes as she looked up at Astra. With frightening calm, she said, "Why didn't you help me when I asked?"

Because I feared to end up as you have—or worse.

"Because . . . I am a coward," Astra said simply, without apology or regret. "I was afraid. I still am."

"Yet you didn't report me. Perhaps I should be grateful—but you're trying to avoid commitment, Astra, either for Portia or against her. How long do you think she will allow that?"

Tressa looked down at the knife again, hefting it—then suddenly threw it at the far wall. As it clattered to the floor, she took in a long deep breath, and Astra could Read her fighting to hold back tears. Anger swallowed Tressa's grief, and Astra knew she would not follow Master Julius to the plane of the dead. Not yet.

There was a Temple of Selene attached to Portia's Academy; Astra had been there many times, playing her lute to the glory of the goddess. Selene protected the chastity of the young female Readers—but she also blessed many young women for the last time at their weddings. Four young girls, Readers in training, were decorating the temple with flowers. They wore pink silk dresses rather than their usual plain white, in honor of the occasion.

A priest and priestess of Selene would officiate at

the ceremony—they were not Readers, so there was no reason for the priest not to enter the Academy grounds. Nor for the bridegroom, now that he had been declared failed. Astra Read him in the ante-room, a sad young man, still bewildered and dis-believing.

He was not Reading; all Astra could tell were his surface emotions. He did not seem curious to Read for his bride—not surprising, for Tressa was also not interested in the man chosen for her. Her shields were up more tightly than Astra had ever known; for all she showed, Tressa might not have been a Reader at all.

Astra wanted to tell her she didn't feel pity—however much she might dislike Tressa, there was no question that she deserved her rank of Magister. Tressa had been treated unfairly—Astra rankled at the injustice, but did not know how to counter it. She had tried before, for Helena. Now she was older, and knew much more than she had then. Now her punishment for disputing Portia's decision would be far worse than being deprived of her music.

But Tressa was right: she could not refuse to take sides forever.

Tressa, she thought, holding her thoughts care-fully inward so no one could Read them, *you will be avenged. I don't know what, but I will do something to help stop this madness!*

It was too late for Tressa, but Astra felt better for her vow to do something before Tressa's fate befell some other Reader. She and Master Claudia hung away Tressa's black-bordered white gown. The black outer robes of her Magister status had already been taken away. On the narrow bed lay the small parcel of clothes Tressa owned which gave no indication of belonging to a Reader.

Tressa returned from her bath. Claudia helped her into her loose underrobe, and sat her down to ar-range her hair. Taming the thick black mass into

chaste braids atop her head took some time, and the
silence among the three women stretched endlessly.

Astra fingered the red marriage gown. It was soft-
est silk, and intrinsically beautiful—if only the bride
were happily choosing to marry a man she loved.
She knew Tressa perceived it as ugly—as she would,
were she forced to wear it to wed a stranger and
destroy her powers.

What would happen, she wondered idly, if the
bride and groom decided not to consummate their
marriage? *Surely* no Master Reader spied on their
wedding bed to make certain—

She almost gagged at the thought.

Yet for all the rumors and innuendos her errant
powers had brought her over the years, never once
had she heard of a couple not performing their mari-
tal duties. Peculiar, when they were always strangers
and usually sick at heart at having been expelled
from the familiar life of the Academy.

A cloying smell assailed her nostrils, and she turned
to see Claudia molding the last stray locks of Tressa's
hair with perfumed oil.

Tressa wrinkled her nose. "Uff! That stuff smells
like Morella's whores!"

Indeed it did, Astra recognized, only stronger, and
with a few subtle musky tones she didn't know.

"Oh—I can't stand that!" Tressa protested. "Let
me go wash it off!"

"No," Master Claudia insisted, one hand on Tressa's
shoulder holding her in place. "It is the traditional
wedding oil. You must wear it, just as your bridegroom does. I mixed it for you myself, Tressa—it is
the formula specified in the wedding rite of Selene."

An aphrodisiac, Astra speculated. Probably intended
to make things easier. Still, her nose wrinkled too as
she brought the red dress and helped Claudia put it
on Tressa.

Then Claudia picked up the token both Astra and
Tressa had been studiously ignoring—a small enamel

badge, black circle on a white background. As she started to pin it to Tressa's dress, the young woman pushed her hand away. "No! Master Claudia, you know I don't deserve—!"

"Oh, child," the older woman said, her eyes brimming with tears, "no Reader thinks she deserves it, but the Council of Masters must make certain that no undeserving Reader reaches the upper ranks. The nonReaders trust us to govern our own."

A surge of sympathy opened Astra's powers despite her intent to keep them under control, and she felt the deep sincerity of Claudia's feelings for Tressa. If there was a conspiracy among the Masters, she was sure the healer was no part of it.

But as she escorted Tressa to the temple, Astra let herself Read for other conspirators. Could she catch someone gloating with satisfaction?

No. There were the girls she taught music, the best of the advanced class, playing sweetly and looking charming in their pink dresses. There were the priest and priestess of Selene, robed in blue and silver.

A privacy screen shielded the door to the anteroom, where the bridegroom waited gloomily, accompanied by two male Masters in their red robes. The Master Readers would Read the ceremony from there, never entering the temple of the Academy of female Readers. Only the groom, on shaking legs, had to walk out to face the assembly.

He, too, was dressed all in red—how ironic, Astra thought, that these two, who had dreamed of wearing the scarlet of Master Readers one day, should end their dreams in the red of marriage garments.

Bride and groom would now see one another for the first time, for neither one had had the desire to Read for the other, both parties enclosed in their private grief. If it was not coincidence, someone had done an amazing job of matching physical types—the young man was slightly taller than Tressa, and had the same thick black hair and black eyes. Astra suspected that when he was in a good mood those eyes would flash just as Tressa's did. Two of a kind. Was it possible that once they were past the difficulties of this forced marriage they would find happiness together?

Astra sincerely hoped that they would.

The ceremony began. The musicians fell silent, and the priest and priestess began chanting to the goddess, first in her incarnation as the goddess of chastity, then as one of the many aspects of the Great Mother.

Astra, stationed behind Tressa, waited for the signal to remove the light bridal veil. As she leaned forward to do so, she came between the bride and groom . . . and smelled the scented oil he also wore.

But the man's was different, pleasant, attractive, drawing her to turn to look at him and realize that he was very handsome indeed—

It is an aphrodisiac! Astra realized, quickly lifting Tressa's veil away and stepping back out of range. Still, she doubted that the powers of that oil could do much against the severe depression of the immediate participants in the ceremony. Neither of them seemed to be attracted to the other—and both were still completely closed to Reading.

They were not allowed to remain so, however. When the priest and priestess completed the wedding prayers, joined the hands of the bride and groom, and had them vow loyalty to the Goddess and to one another, there was only one more step to the ceremony. For nonReaders, that step was merely sharing a goblet of wine, first symbol of the life they would now share.

For Readers, though, the ceremony included the joining of minds as well as hands. Portia herself joined the priestess, Marina beside her with the goblet of wine. The priestess blessed the two Master

Readers, and Portia began something Astra had witnessed only once before, at Helena's wedding.

"Stephano," Portia directed the bridegroom, "open your mind. Read your bride. Tressa, let your thoughts meet those of your husband. Read with me."

There was no denying Portia's command. The bride and groom began to Read, Portia drawing them and every Reader in the temple into a most beautiful soaring emotion. She captured Tressa's wild, prancing thoughts, too spirited to tame—and Stephano's eager quickness, sharp wit, loyal courage.

The bride and groom turned to one another, startled recognition on their faces. To her joy, Astra saw them smile—the Masters had chosen well. Maybe that was why such marriages always seemed to work—

It was impossible to retain independent thought as Portia wove the two personalities together in a dreamlike pattern more compelling than any music Astra had ever heard. No Reader could resist joining in, minds circling the intertwined thoughts Portia manipulated into a promise of shared happiness.

It was far more beautiful than what Astra remembered from Helena's wedding. She had been much younger then, unable to control her own powers at all, totally caught up in what Portia had been able to make of the weaker powers of Helena and Tranos. Stephano must be as strong a Reader as Tressa, for what Portia found to work with today engaged every Reader's mind in a rapture such as—

Astra realized she had withdrawn from the rapport, was observing it from without, admiring but not participating, something she could not do at age twelve. As Portia's thoughts developed, she felt strangely distanced, as if she were watching a drama. But Tressa and Stephano were not acting; for them it was all real, shared love, shared grief, shared joy.

Recognition tingled along Astra's spine. Something she had picked up from Portia—making that poor

mother see her dead baby—making her *see* with a
Reader's inner eye—

Making her see what was not real!

Gooseflesh rose on Astra's body. There had been
no Reader mother . . . now. No mother, no dead
baby—and not a fever dream! A memory Portia had
let slip in a moment of guilt.

And Astra knew, knew as surely as if Portia had
confessed it aloud, that the mother was *her* mother—
that Portia had made Cassandra see Astra, her new-
born infant, dead—so Portia could take the child,
daughter of two strong Readers, and raise her to her
own uses!

*My mother didn't desert me! Portia betrayed her—
betrayed me! My mother loved me, but Portia made
her Read me as dead!*

Just then, "Drink," Portia told the bride and groom,
proffering the goblet.

Astra looked up, fearing to find that Portia had
Read her discovery, but the Master of Masters was
too caught up in what she was doing to notice.

Astra Read within herself to gain control, waiting
until her pounding heart stilled. When she dared
Read outward again, she refused to join in the rapport until she made sure she would not give away
her thoughts. Her anger bubbled up, threatening to
focus on Portia's hypocrisy. She had to calm down!
There was nothing she could do here—nothing she
could do at all until the wedding was over and she
had time to think and plan.

Seeking to fix her mind elsewhere, she Read Tressa
and Stephano directly in front of her. Stephano had
just drunk the spiced wine, and was handing the
goblet to Tressa, who drank deeply. Astra started to
Read Tressa, found her still caught in the rapport
Portia had created, and shied away, her Reading
uncontrolled, everything flowing in on her as she
fought to keep her roiling emotions out of the rapport.

Tressa, reaching for Stephano's hands, dropped

the wine goblet. It still contained some wine, and Astra stepped back by reflex as it splashed toward her white dress.

And as she focused gratefully on the wine, her wild powers Read it, not just wine and spices—but beneath, something else in the wine—

To calm herself, she let curiosity take hold, her Reading powers fixed on the wine pooling on the marble floor. The analytical technique she had learned at Gaeta took over—she recognized the alcohol, cinnamon, a tiny touch of mandragora, and—

Entranced, Astra took apart every ingredient, not realizing, until a murmur and a movement of everyone in the temple recalled her to herself, that Portia had ended the beautiful marriage rapport.

At that very moment, Astra found the last ingredient in the wine, and looked up sharply in horror, to find Portia's eyes on her even as her rebellious mind was telling her something even more terrible than Portia's treachery to one young woman long ago—it was treachery to all the Readers the Master of Masters ordered married off, set on the Path of the Dark Moon by diminishing their powers with—

White lotus!

Chapter Four

Astra fled the temple, fled the Academy grounds, fled from every lie in her life.

Fled from Portia.

In her emotional state, her powers were open to the thoughts of everyone she passed. But she could tolerate that, almost ignore it, as her mind scanned for Readers watching her, following her out of body.

Nothing so far, but—

Only after she was many streets away from the temple did she allow herself to stop and catch her breath.

This is madness! If Portia's the one in the wrong, why am I the one who's running away?

"Because you're a coward, Astra," she muttered to herself, "just as you told Tressa. Portia has the power to destroy you, and now you've given her a reason!"

There had to be someplace to hide, even from the Master of Masters, if only long enough to make a plan. . . .

Zanos! He'd know what to do. But he's got so much to worry about right now, fighting that death match—

Of course! The arena! The last place a Reader would go, especially when blood sports were in progress!

As she approached her destination, the young Reader scanned the arena's medical room. She was not surprised to find a male Magister Reader languishing there, closed to Reading to shut out the carnage going on above him. With any luck, his mind would stay closed, unable to Read any alert Portia might send out in an attempt to find Astra.

She focused her powers on the gladiators' preparation rooms. There was Zanos, getting ready for his match. It had to be coming up soon. She would have to wait until the match was over.

If he survived—

But he has to win! He just has to. I need his help . . . I need him.

The gates to the arena were closed, the seats filled to capacity. The tumultuous roar of the crowd was the loudest Astra had ever heard. She closed herself to Reading as best she could, concentrating on what to do next. Composing herself, she approached the men guarding the gate. "Medical emergency," she said briskly. "Open the gates, please."

Once admitted, she moved quickly to the ramp to the underground area. Above her, the excitement of the crowd was a great tent of mental energy, sheltering her—

An icy touch stabbed at her mind.

Portia!

//You cannot elude me so easily, child,// the Master of Masters told her.

//I'm not a child!// Astra countered, pressing her back against the tunnel wall and shutting her eyes in concentration.

//Nevertheless, I know what's best for you. Come home, Astra. There is no place for you outside the Academy.//

//No! Let me alone!//

The icy touch became a pain, attacking her concentration. Portia was trying to bend her to her will, control her mind by projecting images of pain and fear.

Astra rejected them—but they became more intense. She had no choice; she let herself slip down to the tunnel floor and broke free of the pain by leaving her body.

The bloodlust of the arena crowd was now a familiar horror, but there was a *power* in this collection of emotions that cried out to her frustration and fear. If she could control it, turn it against Portia—

//Astra, listen to me,// Portia demanded. //You don't understand what you Read in the marriage cup—//

//I Read more than just white lotus, Portia. I Read *you*—today, and when I was delirious in the infirmary.// The crowd's fury brought out her own indignation, and her wild talent suddenly told her, //You Read me as I lay close to death, and I reminded you of Cassandra, my mother. You remembered the day of my birth, while she was still weak, her powers blunted—how you deceived her into thinking I was dead!//

Portia gave no reply, for none was necessary—Astra could Read past her shields now, Read everything she was thinking, every conspiracy—

Every murder.

Astra's self-loathing at the way she had turned away from knowing what Portia was doing turned to anger against the Master of Masters.

//Why, Portia? Why did you try to make me part of your schemes?//

//You know why,// the old woman replied. //Child of two strong Masters—you are something unheard of in the history of the Reader system. At the peak of your powers, you could have become the strongest Master Reader who ever lived!//

//And you planned to use me to continue control over the Readers,// Astra realized. //You tried to make me your protégé, but your plan had one flaw. You couldn't take Cassandra's place as my mother because you didn't love me. You don't know how to love—truly love—anybody!//

It was all there in Portia's mind, open to Astra's

powers. The Master of Masters had been born into the Emperor's family, the only person of royal lineage ever to develop a Reader's powers. Once those powers were discovered, how anxious that family had been to pack her off to the Academy, away from the power they intrigued for.

Portia could not show love to Astra because it had never been shown to her.

But Astra had no time for sympathy. Knowing the past did not change the present, and the present could very well end in Astra's death—for she now knew too much.

//Astra, return to your body,// Portia commanded. //Come back to the Academy and let me show you everything that is happening. You know only a few facts. Once you know all, you will understand why we must—

//Not "we"!// Astra told her. //I'm not one of your corrupt Masters, or one of your hired killers—like Vortius! He killed Master Quantus at your order! *That* was what you were afraid I'd Read in your office that day—the day you assigned me the arena as punishment!//

The death match in the arena was approaching its climax. The crowd rose to its feet, screaming for the death stroke. Waves of emotion crashed over both Readers, dragging them into an undertow of frenzy. But both Master and Magister fought them off, locked in a battle of wills.

Suddenly Portia's mind sought to grapple directly with Astra's, to make her forget all she had learned about the conspiracy—

But the hypnotic techniques that worked on nonReaders could be eluded by another Reader—if she was strong enough.

For the first time in her life, Astra fought back, turning her anger outward instead of letting frustration eat at her from inside.

The crowd's roar increased, the waves becoming a

flood. They pounded Astra on one side as Portia's attack bombarded her from another—she couldn't fight them both!

Instinctively, she embraced the fury of the crowd, concentrated it through her own talent, and hurled it at Portia.

The Master could not retain her shields against such strength.

Astra's hope stirred—Portia would leave the arena, return to her body at the Academy, and Astra would be able to escape.

But Portia had not climbed to her position or held it for so long by giving up.

Somehow, she fought off the bloodlust and threw it back at Astra.

But the younger woman was quick to learn. She opened to the frenzy, took its echo from Portia, combined phantom with reality—and hurled both together at the Master of Masters on the spear of a gladiator's death agony.

Portia's mental scream was lost in the din of the arena crowd. Astra felt her fall away from the conflict, Read her return to her own body, defeated . . . and just barely alive.

The crowd was cheering the victor, but Astra found no joy in her triumph.

Blessed gods! I was only defending myself! I didn't want to kill her!

But a part of her was not so sure. How much of that bloodlust had belonged to the crowd . . . and how much was hers?

Astra Read Master Marina rush into Portia's private chamber to discover the old woman unconscious. Terrified that her emotions might reveal her presence, Astra withdrew from the scene. The return to her hastily abandoned body was agony. Every joint screamed as she rolled over onto her hands and knees, then slowly forced herself to her feet. She felt dizzy, but her mind was clearing. There was still no one else in the tunnel, thank the gods, so her body had been in no real danger.

But now all of me is in danger, she thought bitterly. *If Portia recovers—*

She hadn't won anything. The Council of Masters and the Emperor would have her either exiled as a traitor—or executed as a threat to the state.

Oh, Zanos!

Almost involuntarily her mind reached out to find him in the arena, sword and shield at the ready, squaring off against his opponent.

Mallen was everything she had feared—bigger and heavier than Zanos, with black beard and hair so long that he looked like a savage. Astra Read both of them . . . and gasped as both men braced themselves—and became unReadable!

Mallen outsized him by half a head and considerable weight, but that didn't bother Zanos. His main concern was how to put on a show for the spectators.

Despite his secret advantage, he must beware the unexpected. Any freak mishap could endanger him— like twisting his ankle or letting Mallen past his guard in overconfidence. That was how he had received the wound he had relied on all these years as an excuse to protect his powers. Serafon had healed then what no Aventine healer could have . . . but she had no powers to raise the dead.

The babble of the spectators hushed with anticipation as the two fighters warily circled each other. The net in Mallen's left hand didn't bother Zanos as much as the trident in his opponent's right. He had a mild contempt for spear weapons in arena combat, but its three deadly points couldn't be ignored. Mallen had the look of a man confident of victory. That would soon be gone—but what was it about him that seemed vaguely familiar?

Mallen tested Zanos with several feints, using both seine and trident. Zanos obliged him by lightly dodging each move, gauging Mallen's quickness. *He's fast for his size*, Zanos thought, *and saving his best moves for later*.

He countered with several moves of his own, noting that Mallen didn't backstep very smoothly. That meant a rush attack would—

Mallen leaped unexpectedly at Zanos, catching his sword blade between two trident points, swinging the net overhead in a wide arc.

It seemed to open like a giant hand, reaching out to grab Zanos' head and shoulders.

He ducked under Mallen's left arm and brought up his shield with a stiff-armed blow that connected with Mallen's jaw, knocking him backwards as Zanos pulled his sword free.

"Very good, red-hair," Mallen said beneath the applause of the spectators. He smiled as his left fist wiped the blood off his lip and into his beard. "Very good indeed."

Zanos' eyes widened. Mallen had said those last three words in Maduran!

He studied Mallen's face as they circled, dodging almost by reflex. Mallen smiled again—about to take Zanos' head off with the trident.

Zanos let his powers deflect the weapon's course, but the nearest point grazed his right temple.

He suppressed a cry more of surprise than pain, and spun away from the attack, following through with a sword swing at Mallen's right side as the large man rushed past him. The blow bounced harmlessly off his opponent's armor.

Zanos pulled himself together, putting his right thumb to the wound, Adeptly stopping the blood. *He spoke Maduran to throw you off guard*, he told himself, *and it worked! A trick you don't expect the rawest trainee to fall for. He couldn't be from home—*

Couldn't he? As they squared off again, Zanos recalled his homeland before he had been kidnapped at the age of eight. There were stories about black-haired tribes who lived above the mountain snow line, fierce warriors who had once waged war against his people, and lost. He had accepted the stories as bedtime tales spun by his father for him and his younger brother. But they could be true—

Mallen charged again, swinging the net over his head like a whip. *He's very good with that thing,* Zanos thought as he stepped forward, timing an attack to Mallen's midsection.

Suddenly the net flew from Mallen's hand. Once again it seemed to spread of its own accord. No one Zanos had ever seen could make it perform that way one-handed!

He couldn't dodge the seine, so he concentrated, twisting the net into a smaller shape, batting it away with his shield.

But Mallen was on him with the trident, blocking out the sun. Shield met trident as Zanos aimed a thrust at Mallen's left side, intending to wound him.

Sword tip bounced away from leather armor after striking solid air.

Zanos' moment of puzzlement was just long enough for Mallen's left fist to come down on his right shoulder, close to his neck. The blow nearly drove him to his knees—but from the advantage of his bent position, as Mallen prepared for a second blow, Zanos butted Mallen in the stomach with his head, knocking the wind out of him.

The crowd cheered for more, but each fighter was momentarily staggered, seeking to breathe and rest. Zanos tested his tingling arm—his shoulder was bruised, but the collarbone had not broken.

Mallen's youth gave his breath back quickly. He made a move toward his net.

I can't let him wear me down, Zanos realized. *I'll have to finish him off quickly, or he'll simply outlast me.* He jumped to cut Mallen off.

The black-haired giant laughed as he backstepped, shifting his trident to a two-handed grip. Using it

like a quarterstaff, Mallen feinted twice, then swung
the blunt end at Zanos' ribs, under his guard. Zanos
deflected the blow's force, letting it barely touch him
as he rolled away.

*He's playing with me. He thinks he can keep me
running until I'm tired—but I have advantages he
doesn't know about.*

He dodged another blow, came up with his sword—
and distinctly felt the tug of something he could not
see swing the blade away from Mallen's unprotected
thigh!

He's countering with powers of his own!

"I thought so," Mallen said softly. "From the moment I first heard about you, the great undefeated
gladiator, I knew you had to be like me—a secret
Adept."

"Are you from Madura?" Zanos asked in his native
tongue. By the gods—could this man be as eager to
return home as Zanos was?

"Indeed, red-hair," Mallen replied in the same
language. He twirled the trident into an underhand
grip, aiming the points at Zanos. "Unlike you, I
came to this land as a man, and of my own free will,
knowing I could prosper with my powers."

"But why?" Zanos feinted a sword thrust, then
retreated a step. "This is a land of evil!"

Mallen began circling him. "Our homeland is a
place of greater evil! The meager powers you and I
have are nothing to those of the rulers of Madura. To
have stayed in the islands would have meant my
death . . . or something far worse," he added, then
spun and dived, shoulder-rolling past the net and
coming up with it in his left hand, to the applause of
the crowd.

Zanos cursed his carelessness, and felt something
else. Fear. The fear he had not felt since his early
days in the arena. For the first time since he had
learned to control his powers, he was in a genuinely
even match.

Or was it even? What if Mallen's powers were stronger?

He didn't want to kill Mallen—he wanted to ask him about Madura. What was happening there now? Had anyone from his village survived the raid in which he had been taken—had it been rebuilt? Were there people who could teach him to use his Adept powers more efficiently? What were the terrible things being done by the present rulers?

All Zanos' memories, even though they were from the perspective of a small boy, recalled a land benevolently ruled by powerful Adepts who called the rain but held off storms, to make their islands green and bountiful. Adepts who healed the sick and injured, and—at least so the children had whispered to one another—had learned the secret of life itself.

"Mallen—I must talk with you—"

"Talk!" The bigger man laughed, guarding himself with the trident as he shook out the seine. "You're not going to talk to anybody, Zanos the Gladiator—you are going to *die*. You recognize where my powers come from. You cannot live to tell your friend the Emperor!"

An invisible fist clutched at Zanos' heart. He staggered, using his own powers to ease the pressure and dissipate the pain—and saw in Mallen's eyes that the man would do whatever was necessary to rid himself of the danger Zanos presented.

But neither of us can kill at a distance, or the spectators will get suspicious.

The crowd was screaming for action—any kind of action—furious that the two gladiators were still circling and feinting. They wanted blood. *And they don't care whose.*

Sensing Mallen preparing to try for a deathblow, Zanos charge-attacked first, swinging his sword in wide arcs. Mallen set himself, timing Zanos' approach as he poised his trident and flicked the net back and forth like a writhing snake.

Two steps from striking distance, Zanos drew his arm back for a prodigious swing that would take Mallen's head from his shoulders.

As he felt Mallen's powers start to deflect the blow, Zanos twisted his wrist and put Adept power behind his effort, guiding the blade past Mallen's face and straight through the wooden shaft of the trident. His shoulder collided with Mallen's chest, and the two men went down sprawling.

The crowd leaped to its feet, screaming as the fighters leaped up, a few paces apart.

Mallen now held just a wooden pole in his right hand, hefting it to find its new center of balance.

But Zanos was on his feet—ready to end this match now.

Mallen tossed the pole high over his head.

Expecting it was some Adept trick, Zanos followed its upward flight for a moment—just long enough for Mallen's net to leap out and wrap itself around his sword.

As Zanos slashed at the net with the sharp edge, his sword hilt was suddenly too hot to handle!

His grip loosened by reflex, and Mallen's net yanked the blade out of his hand. It landed at his opponent's feet, and when Mallen picked it up it was obviously no longer hot.

He knows what to do with the powers he has! Zanos thought, and tried to apply his own powers to the sword—but Mallen broke his concentration with a frenzied assault, discarding the net to use a two-handed grip on the sword, battering away at Zanos' shield.

The screams of the spectators became deafening as they sensed the approaching climax—and the crowning of a new champion.

I won't give in! Zanos thought as he deflected blow after blow, slowly retreating beneath Mallen's onslaught. He set himself and charged Mallen with the shield, but succeeded only in throwing him back a step.

The crowd cheered Zanos' bravery, but it was clear they thought he had lost.

It was not in him to accept defeat!

Again he struck at Mallen with the shield—only to be driven back once more, until his foot struck something half-buried in the sand—

Deliberately, he fell to one knee, giving Mallen the advantage. The crowd shrieked anticipation.

Using a lateral swing, Mallen knocked the shield from Zanos' grip, sending him sprawling. With a cry of triumph, Mallen towered over him, sword raised for the death stroke as Zanos scrambled to his knees—

Mallen's victory cry became a scream of pain as Zanos' clasped hands came up right where his armor separated when he raised his arms—

The sword fell as Mallen clutched futilely at the cut-off shaft of the trident head now sticking out of his chest.

Zanos backed off as Mallen sank to his knees, blood spurting from chest and mouth.

For one long moment, a look passed between the two men. Then one slowly fell on his side as the other rose to his feet.

Zanos stared at the corpse for a long time, only slowly becoming aware of the cheers from the stands all around him. He looked, unseeing, at the blood on his hands, and then at the nodding smile of the Emperor.

Feeling numb and very tired, the Maduran bowed for the last time to the leader of his captors as they cheered the undefeated champion . . . cheered his first true arena victory.

Zanos was besieged with congratulations and offers to buy him victory drinks before he even reached the medical room. Some of his fighters had to clear a path for him and keep out the well-wishers while he was being examined.

The stiff silence of the Reader who cleansed and

bandaged his wounds was a welcome relief. Zanos waited until he and two of his men were leaving the stadium before allowing himself to think about Astra, let himself wonder where she was and when she'd hear about his victory. Part of him wished she were here to share his joy, but that would have to wait until tomorrow, after he'd recovered his strength through a good meal and a long night of healing sleep.

He hadn't seen Ard since the match began, just after he'd entrusted his servant with his personal seal and the gold for wagering.

"No need to worry, Master," Aeson said. "As soon as you won, Ard went to collect your winnings. Salamis and Massos are helping him carry all that gold back to your villa. Not a legion of thieves would dare try to rob *them!*"

Fine. Zanos could trust Ard to see he wasn't cheated. Soon Ard and Lanna would no longer be his servants, but fellow countrymen, journeying back to Madura with him. He could hardly wait till it was safe to tell them of his powers—but not until they were all on board the ship he would soon own, with the empire at their backs. *Tomorrow,* he thought with satisfaction, *I can start turning my dream into a real plan for getting out of here.*

And he deliberately put out of his mind Mallen's description of Madura.

A victorious gladiator, especially one who had received no serious injury, was expected to celebrate. Zanos usually enjoyed such parties, but today's combat had drained his Adept energies more than he had first realized. By the time he had made a brief appearance at his third party, he was fighting heavy fatigue, moving little better than a sleepwalker.

Some of the partygoers made jokes about the gladiator having too much wine, but he had drunk no more than a swallow or two, while restraining himself from eating more than his share of the food set out. He was content to let them believe what they wanted as he stumbled toward his villa, supported by two of his fighters. His home was almost in sight when a mob of his friends seemed to descend out of nowhere, sweeping him along to the house of Gareth, one of the other stable owners.

Despite his weary protests, he was put in a thronelike chair at the head of a table. It was all he could do to stay awake and acknowledge the praise heaped upon him by those who'd won heavily on his victory.

Eventually he became aware of a new group of guests—Morella and her girls, wearing their prettiest clothes and best painted faces.

The party quickly turned to something approaching an orgy, giving Zanos the perfect excuse to make his exit. Standing up, however, proved to be a little difficult, and the door seemed a hundred miles away. Morella and one of her girls appeared beside him, each slipping under one of his arms to give him the support he needed. Morella made some joke about a sleepy little boy needing to be put to bed, and he managed a weak smile as they drifted out of the noisy warmth of Gareth's house and into the quiet coolness of the street.

Some time later, he was lowered into his bed and his sandals removed. It felt good to have such friends— but they weren't his usual friends. They smelled too good.

Was he in danger? No . . . but still something felt . . . *wrong* . . . somewhere in his world.

Whatever it was, it would have to wait until morning. A light blanket slowly settled over his torso as his last strength faded, lowering him into dreamless sleep.

"By Mawort's golden blade!"
Zanos' swearing woke Astra from her fitful sleep. As she sat up in the gladiator's bed, he jumped out of

it. She could Read guilty fear in him, then puzzlement as he realized that he was still fully dressed, and so was she—

As a prostitute.

"Astra?" He became unReadable again as he squinted at her painted face. "Is that you?"

"Yes, Zanos," she said solemnly. "I'm sorry I startled you. I forgot about this stuff on my face. I didn't expect to fall asleep, but I lay down here because I was almost as weary as you were. Morella and I all but carried you here from Gareth's house."

"But what are you doing here?" he demanded. "And why are you dressed like that?"

"I had no place else to go. My life as a Reader is over."

Zanos sat down on the edge of the bed, facing her, as she told him what she had discovered at Tressa's wedding.

"White lotus?" he asked. "Given to a Reader? But Astra, it just doesn't make sense to addict all the Readers on the Path of the Dark Moon—there isn't enough of the stuff in the whole empire to serve the craving of so many people. I could understand addicting your friend if she were *not* being failed—if she were going to be forced to do someone's dirty work, like Darien and Primus."

Astra did not correct his assumption that Tressa was her friend—if it hadn't been for Astra's cowardice, by this time she should have been. Instead . . .

"It wasn't the addictive form," she explained.

"What?" Zanos asked in obvious confusion. "White lotus is the most addictive drug I know of."

"Yes, in the form distilled directly from the plant. But I learned in my medical training about derivatives which retain the power to make a patient highly suggestible, but cause no later craving. They are used to treat patients with mind sickness. I had only the most basic of such training, as my talents lie in music, not healing—but I did learn about the existence of such drugs. Zanos, right now I'm not certain how much I learned from Portia's mind and how much I have pieced together, but this is what I know:

"Sometimes Readers who fail to reach the highest ranks are given a white lotus derivative in their marriage wine. The Master Reader performing the ceremony then implants the suggestion not only that husband and wife will be completely happy with one another, but that their Reading powers will be permanently reduced when they consummate their marriage."

"You mean without drugs they're not?" he asked in shock.

"Yes, they are—or I think they are. But how much or how permanently, I don't know. Zanos, they're failing Master Readers with years of experience. That's not the way the Academy system is supposed to operate—but it's happening. Even supposing the effect of consummating a marriage were to reduce the powers of a Master to those of a Magister Reader—those are still highly significant powers! Such a person, resentful of what had happened, could be a serious threat to the Council of Masters."

"I see," Zanos said, fingering the stubble of beard on his chin. "So they make certain such strong Readers do lose most of their powers." He shuddered. "They deliberately cripple them, as some people will lame a slave to keep him from running away."

Astra nodded. "I have another piece of information, from years ago—before the corruption in the Council of Masters, I think. My mother was not married to my father. Her powers were so diminished by my birth that Portia was able to make her think her baby had died—yet she recovered enough within a few days to escape from an Academy full of Readers. In fact, she vanished so thoroughly that she was never found. Neither was my father."

"That's what Portia told you," Zanos said flatly. "I

don't want to hurt you, Astra—but isn't it more likely that they were quietly . . . executed?"

"No!" she protested. "No—that's one of the things I Read from Portia. They escaped across the border. I suppose . . . that means if they were ever discovered to be Readers the savages killed them. But maybe they're still alive out there somewhere—maybe they escaped beyond the savage lands to the north, and found some other part of the world where Readers are treated kindly. At least I'd like to think so."

He smiled gently. "I hope you're right. But how could you have learned so much from Portia's mind? Surely the Master of Masters doesn't leave her thoughts open for a Magister Reader to eavesdrop on?"

Lowering her eyes, she described her battle with the Master of Masters, ashamed now of how viciously she had struck out at the old woman, yet still unable to think of any other way she could have saved herself. "I'm gambling that Portia won't regain consciousness for hours," she said. "The fact that I'm still alive and free means that I was right. But when she wakens she'll either alert the entire Reader system to find me, or send out Vortius and his killers!"

"Or both," muttered Zanos. But then he put a reassuring hand on her shoulder. "Don't worry. I'll find a way to protect you. Now I see why you're dressed like that—you figured that one of Morella's girls going home with me wouldn't draw any attention." A wry smile curved his lips. "I'll tell you the irony of *that* some other time. Right now, we must get you out of Tiberium—"

"No, Zanos. It's much more complicated than that."

"I know. You have to get out of the empire entirely. And yes, Astra, there *are* places beyond the lands of the savages. Thanks to my winnings from yesterday's match, I'll soon leave this land too. Come with me and my friends. We'll find a way to hide you for the week or so—"

"That's what I'm trying to tell you! You don't *have* a week or so. You have to get out of the empire this very day, before some other Reader scans you!"

He slowly withdrew his hand from her shoulder. "What are you saying?" he asked, a cold, deadly tone in his voice. Astra was suddenly aware that this man had made a career of killing people.

This was the moment she had dreaded. She grasped his retreating hand and held it tightly. "Zanos, please . . . hear me out. I Read your match with Mallen— and I discovered the secret you two shared. I thanked every god in the universe when you defeated him . . . and only then thought to wonder if you were an Adept spy for the savages." His hand closed painfully on hers, but she continued with forced calm, "I know you can't be."

"What makes you so sure?"

"The savages hate and fear all Readers they don't control. If you were one of them, you wouldn't have jeopardized your mission by using your powers to save my life when I was so ill." His grip on her hand eased, and she could almost have laughed at the surprise on his face.

"Yes," she told him, "I recognized you. I dreamed about the Sun God, but when I discovered that you had Adept powers, I realized that the god with the flaming hair in my delirium was you. And only some-one who cared about me would risk using such pow-ers where any one of a hundred Readers could have discovered and exposed him." Astra gently pressed his hand against her cheek. "Thank you," she whis-pered.

Zanos shook his head, smiling at her. "I always feared somebody would discover my secret, and could never imagine what would happen next. But you're not just anybody. You've become the most important person in the world to me. When I heard that you were so ill, I could not stay away—not when I knew I could heal you."

"I know," she replied. "Now it's my turn to help you. Something happened during your match with Mallen. By the time it was over, whatever trick you'd been using to hide your powers stopped working. You remained unReadable. The gods were smiling on you, for the Magister in the medical room only Read your wounds. I was carefully Reading him all the time you were in there, but there was nothing I could have done if he had tried to scan your thoughts—"

"He must have been a friend of Darien and Primus." Zanos shrugged. "He didn't even want to look at me, much less treat my injuries. But now that I've had a night's sleep to recover my strength—"

"You're *still* unReadable, Zanos. There was only one moment when you woke up," she told him, "when I could catch your feelings—and then it blanked out. What happened in the arena yesterday somehow changed you—increased your powers beyond your ability to hide them. If any Reader—even one on the Path of the Dark Moon—were to try to Read you right now, your secret would be out."

"And I'd have to fight off a mob to get out of the city," he concluded. "But there has to be something we can do. I need time to finish the deal with the owner of the *Nightwind*."

"A merchant ship?"

"A smuggler's ship, actually. War or no war, the Emperor still needs fishing ships for his food and smuggling ships to get him soap and spices. That's why certain vessels have not been conscripted for the invasion fleet. The Nightwind's owner has had money problems lately, and is open to accepting a rather large bribe—"

A worried look crossed his face as he stopped.

"What's wrong?" she asked.

"I just realized what was strange when you and Morella put me to bed last night." He went to the door and opened it. "Ard! Lanna!"

There was no reply. Astra Read throughout the villa, and found no one. When she told Zanos, he asked, "Did you see either of them last night?"

"Ard let us in. I'm sure he didn't recognize me, although he did stare—but I don't remember seeing Lanna."

Muttering an oath, Zanos strode to the bedroom's west wall. It was painted with a mural of birds in flight, divided into panels. Zanos pressed two spots in one panel and it instantly sprang open, revealing a closetlike hiding place.

He let out a long breath, obviously relieved as he pulled out a small wooden chest, one of three hidden there. "For a moment I was afraid that Ard had betrayed me and run off with my winnings," he said as he lifted the heavy box to a small table. "And I've always been afraid that one of Vortius' corrupt Readers would locate that secret panel."

A sudden pounding at the front door drew Astra's attention away from the chest. She Read through the door—and gasped as she recognized, "It's Vortius!"

"What's he doing here?" Zanos asked, already heading out of the room.

"Zanos—"

"Yes, I know," he said, putting a silencing finger to his lips as he pulled the door shut behind him. With her inner vision, Astra followed him to the front door and watched him admit Vortius, his two bodyguards, and a middle-aged man in the robes of a magistrate. Zanos welcomed the official with a measure of respect, ignoring the gambler and his two thugs.

"I'll come straight to the point, Zanos," said the magistrate. "Vortius claims you are unable or unwilling to pay off the gambling debt you incurred yesterday. He says you owe him nine hundred gold marks."

"Is this some kind of joke?" Zanos shot an angry look at the smug gambler. "I don't owe you a thing."

"You can't lie your way out of it, Zanos," Vortius

retorted, pulling documents out of the folds of his cloak. "You wagered one thousand marks on the outcome of your match yesterday, but put up only a hundred marks at the gambling center. That is permitted, but now you must pay the rest."

"Now I *know* you've gone insane!" Zanos exclaimed. "First of all, I bet only one hundred marks, and second, I *won!*"

"Yes, I know you won," the magistrate said, "which puzzles me all the more. Why did you wager against yourself?"

Zanos snatched the documents from Vortius' hands. Astra bit her lower lip as she Read the unbelievable: a wagering agreement between Zanos and Vortius for one thousand gold marks—on Mallen. The line for the bettor's identification bore the mark of Zanos' personal seal.

"Forgery!" the gladiator exclaimed. "This is fraud—"

"On the contrary," said the magistrate, "I was witness to the transaction; your manservant made this wager as he always does, and finalized it with your seal. You did entrust him to place that bet for you?"

"Not *that* bet! Not against me! Why would I bet against myself in a death match?"

"Oh, come now, Zanos," Vortius sneered. "It's happened before: the heavy favorite makes a deal with his opponent. The favorite is 'defeated' with a slight wound, and he and his friends get rich by betting against him. You were the clear favorite yesterday, but something must have gone wrong between you and Mallen. You were forced to change your plans and kill—"

"That's a lie!" Zanos declared.

None of this makes sense, Astra thought. *If Zanos "lost" the bet, then what's in these—?*

Rocks! Incredulously, Astra Read that the chest on the table was filled not with gold, but with stones. So were the other two. *Ard betrayed him*, she realized, feeling sick. *Oh, Zanos . . .*

"You know the gambling laws, Zanos," the magistrate was saying. "If you cannot pay the debt by noon today, then the state will seize your properties and turn them over to Vortius, after the appropriate taxes have been deducted. And if the assessments show that the value of your properties does not fully cover the debt—"

"—which I'm sure it doesn't," Vortius put in.

"—then you will be turned over to Vortius as his bondservant, to work off the rest."

Zanos tore apart the documents and made a leap for Vortius' throat. The two bodyguards grabbed the gladiator's arms, barely able to restrain him.

//Zanos, no!// Astra projected, even though she knew he couldn't receive her thoughts. If Zanos unleased his powers on four men, including a government official, that mob he feared might consist of half the empire!

For a few brief moments, Zanos became Readable, and Astra could sense his struggle to regain his composure.

"Bondservant!" he spat. "That's just another word for *slave*! I'll never be your slave, Vortius!"

"You will do as the law directs." The gambler smiled. "Or you will find yourself sold into the galleys. Besides, working for me is not so bad. I can be quite generous. After all, I could have pressed my claim last night, and spoiled your celebration."

That's a lie, Astra's powers told her. *Vortius had to be someplace else last night, and couldn't have pressed his claim, even if he'd wanted to.*

But where had he been? She knew that the answer to that question was very important, but Vortius annoyingly would not think of it so she could Read it.

"You have three hours to get your affairs in order, Zanos," the magistrate said. "We will return at noon, and if you do not have the money at hand, all that you own—including your stable of fighters—will be confiscated."

The magistrate left, followed by the gambler. The two thugs released Zanos and followed their master out the door. The gladiator slammed it shut behind them, then closed his eyes and pressed his forehead against it, not moving . . . not even when Astra approached and gingerly touched his shoulder.

"There's no gold in those chests, is there?" he asked.

"I'm sorry," she whispered. "There must be something I can do to help—"

Zanos whirled around, glaring at the bedroom. The small bedside table exploded into pieces, sending the wooden chest crashing to the floor. It split open on impact, spilling stones in all directions.

"Zanos, please! Calm down!"

Slowly the anger drained from his face. "Let's sit down," he said. "I've got to think."

They sat in the kitchen, for Zanos suddenly realized that he was very hungry, a delayed reaction from yesterday. He consumed eggs, bread, cheese, fruit—anything that didn't take much preparation. Astra sat across from him, nibbling on a piece of cheese while she stared at him intently.

As he satisfied his body's needs, his mind ran in circles, searching for a way to pick up the pieces of his shattered dream.

"Why do you have to bribe the captain of the *Nightwind*?" Astra interrupted his thoughts. "Can't you just buy a passage on a merchant ship headed north?"

He shook his head. "One of the things I hate most about this empire is that freedmen have different laws than natural-born citizens. A freedman is not allowed to leave the empire without applying for permission and proving that his business is not to go home. If former slaves could reach their homelands, they might reveal some of the slavers' kidnapping tricks, and make it more difficult to obtain slaves for the empire. A freedman can't even become a merchant sailor or fisherman unless he has a family in the empire—in other words, hostages—to make sure he remains a loyal citizen.

"Besides, I don't have any money now. And all the ships of honest merchants are part of the war fleet, launching in a day or two." He slammed the table with his fist. "I can't believe that Ard and Lanna would do this to me! In less than a month, they would've been free and on their way back home."

"Perhaps Vortius threatened them into betraying you," Astra suggested.

"No. Ard created the pretense of safeguarding my 'winnings.' My trust allowed him to get away with it. He arranged things so that there would be plenty of time for him and Lanna to flee—probably to Vortius' town house." He let out a short, angry laugh. "When I woke up this morning, I thought I had about a week left to my enslavement in this land. Then you told me I had to reduce it to less than a day. Now, thanks to Vortius, I have less than three hours to get you, me, and my friends out of Tiberium."

"But where will we go?" she asked.

"North. Across the border and through the savage lands. The border is four days' ride from here. By the time we cross it, the Aventine army will be invading the savages' west coast. The Adepts will be too busy moving against them to worry about our little group. We should be able to avoid the battleground and reach a port in the far north. Once we get there, we'll do whatever is necessary to get on a ship to Madura. . . . What's wrong?" he asked at the strange look on Astra's face.

"I—I guess I'm just finding it hard to believe this is happening. I can't go back to the Academy; I have to go with you. I never dreamed of any man wanting me—"

He reached across the table for her hand. "I want you and need you, Astra. Even without the danger to our lives and freedom, I couldn't have left without you." He realized this even as he spoke, hoping she could Read how true it was. "But I can't let you come without knowing that the greatest dangers may face us when we reach our destination." He started to tell her what Mallen had said in the arena.

"Yes, I Read both of you during the combat, and could make out most of what you were saying," she said. "What do you think he meant by a 'great evil' forcing him to leave Madura rather than face death or 'something far worse'?"

"I don't know. It could mean a number of things, including slavery," he said. "But I believe that renegade Portia confronted was right—there's nothing we can't do, combining our powers." He wondered, suddenly, if she understood just how he yearned to "combine" with her. And whether she had heard the rumors he had deliberately spread. . . .

What if her idea of their relationship was considerably different from his?

"Astra," he began, "like you, I've had to remain celibate in order to protect my special abilities. When people noticed that I didn't celebrate my victories like most gladiators, I . . . invented an excuse. I let it be known that a wound I received early in my arena career had left me impotent."

Astra nodded. "I heard that story, and believed it . . . until that day I watched you training for the match. You were so strong, so appealing, that I . . ." She blushed a deep scarlet, unable to look at him. "I Read you. Thoroughly."

Zanos laughed, a good hearty laugh that helped to ease his pain. He came around the table, gently lifted Astra to her feet, and hugged her.

"And when I discovered the truth," she added as

she let her arms slide around him, "I didn't know what to think."

"No, but I can imagine," he chuckled. It felt so good to have someone with whom he could share his secrets besides—

Serafon! By Mawort, he'd nearly forgotten that he had to get to her, tell her that all their plans had been upset!

"What's wrong?" Astra asked at his sudden sobriety.

"Nothing. It's just that we have much to do and very little time in which to do it." He gently touched her cheeks and looked into her eyes. "Astra, you never actually said that you would come with me, face the dangers—"

"Oh, yes, my love." She smiled. "I'll journey with you to the ends of the world and beyond, and face the dark gods themselves if they should stand in our way!"

He kissed her then, for the first time—and as she clung to him he felt a kind of strength he'd never before experienced. Over the years, he had eased his natural yearnings by convincing himself that love was, for him, a dangerous weakness. He was glad to discover he'd been wrong.

They spent the next hour hurriedly packing what they thought they would need for the journey. Zanos' plan now called for nine people to travel together— Astra, Serafon, Zanos, and his six fighters. Astra pointed out that the larder held not a day's supply of food for so many.

"And who is Serafon?" she asked.

"High priestess of the Temple of Hesta," Zanos replied. "Like me, she's an Adept, but her powers are strongest 'in the realm of nature,' as she puts it. For many years, she's been secretly helping the farmers around Tiberium, doing what she can to change the weather in their favor. She knows more about living off the land than the rangers of the deep forests. Without her guidance, I would have been dead long ago—executed for trying to escape, or exposed as an Adept."

"But how did—" Astra stopped in midsentence, staring at something beyond the villa wall. "Zanos, we're being watched. An old man in the alley across the street. He's pretending to be asleep, but he's watching this house!"

Zanos slid over to a front window and peeked through the shutter. "That's Varan," he muttered. "Looks like I owe you an apology—you were right that Varan frightened Clea into running away. Vortius is using him to deliver messages now—and his message to me is that I am being watched."

"No," the Reader said as she moved close to him, keeping clear of the window. "Vortius is punishing him with assignments like this because he said something to Clea—he let slip that he's associated with Vortius! Vortius wanted to use Clea again, but she ran the moment Varan tried to approach her—he's thinking right now about how he didn't handle her right . . . because Morella's coming up the street! Phaeru's with her, and they're coming here."

Zanos concentrated in Varan's direction for a moment, and the old man slumped over. "Now he really *is* asleep," he said, "and will stay that way for quite a while. Tell me—how did you get Morella and her girls to help you disguise yourself for Gareth's party last night?"

"I told her our lives were in danger, and that I had to speak with you without Vortius knowing about it. Morella hates Vortius as much as you do, but she has to deal with him and his men anyway. When she told her girls that you were in danger, they immediately volunteered to help. Morella knew about Gareth's party, and he certainly didn't object to some of her girls helping to keep his guests happy."

When Morella knocked at the door, Zanos was already moving to let her in. Both Morella and Phaeru had been crying, but he waited for them to tell him what was wrong.

"Astra told me what you and your girls did to help us last night," he said as he led them to the music room. "I don't know how to thank you."

"Friends help friends, Zanos." She looked at Astra, then back at him. "It's all over The Maze that Vortius is claiming your property and freedom for gambling debts—I take it he somehow cheated you?"

"Somehow," Zanos replied.

"That viper! He's got all the local law in his pocket—I hope you're planning to run rather than try to fight him. Astra, we brought you some clothes suitable for traveling. I know you can't go back to your Academy—"

"How did you know?" she asked.

"Readers aren't the only ones who know things—as soon as I heard about Vortius and Zanos, I realized that you'd been caught in that corruption trying to help your friend. And you're not the first I've helped escape enemies in Tiberium." Tears welled up in Morella's eyes. "I only wish Clea had trusted me to help her this time!"

"Clea?" asked Zanos. "You know where she is?"

"Word reached me this morning. Yesterday, a farmer in the southlands was tilling his field for spring planting. He found her . . . remains. She's been dead for weeks—had to be identified by the rings she was so fond of wearing."

Phaeru turned away with a choked sob.

"She must have been trying to go home—her parents' home is the southlands," Morella went on. "If I could get my hands on the monster who caught up with her—"

"I'm sorry," Astra whispered, remembering Clea's courage in breaking her addiction to white lotus.

"I wish we could do something to help," Zanos added.

"The best thing you two can do is get out of this

corrupt land," Morella said firmly. "Now tell me what Phaeru and I can do to help."

"And just what kind of help are they giving you?" Serafon asked.

"I gave them what money I had left," Zanos told her. "They're buying us horses and supplies. I don't know what to do about my fighters—"

"Don't worry about them," the high priestess said. "They're happy as gladiators. If you *had* been able to free them, you would have done better to encourage them to join the army, for the chance to gain glory in battle. None of your fighters are from Madura, Zanos. All along, you've failed to consider that living in the far north might not suit those not born there. I was hoping you would come to realize that."

Zanos swallowed hard. "Meaning that you would prefer to stay here—and that I shouldn't take Astra?"

"I'm too old to make such changes in my life. Even if I survived the journey, I'm too old to start life over in a strange land." She turned to look at Astra, who had been listening without comment. "And I only partly understand why you are so willing to go with him."

The Reader gave that smile which so intrigued Zanos. "With all due respect, Priestess Serafon, I think you do understand. You have loved and helped Zanos for most of his life. My feelings are very similar, and just as deep." She linked her arm with his, and he let their fingers intertwine as she continued, "I've already told him that I am willing to go anywhere with him, share any danger that threatens him—"

"And risk losing your powers?" Serafon asked.

"We have discussed that," Zanos said. "Since we don't know what enemies we may face in Madura, we will remain celibate until we find a place that is safe to live in. We will consummate our love only after we are wed to one another in a proper Maduran ceremony."

"Which you may not live to see, if you leave here unprepared," the priestess said firmly. "There are so many things I wish I could explain. I have never had a husband, but I have married many couples, and seen the changes that happen to them in a brief space of time. But with the powers you two possess—Zanos, I have only one piece of counsel for you, and Astra, I would like to give you Hesta's blessing. Let me marry you, in the temple, right now. I cannot expect you to understand fully why I must do this, but as the two of you grow to become one, the meaning will become clear."

Zanos was puzzled, but never in his life had Serafon given him bad advice. A glance at Astra told him that she was willing to do as he chose.

Without another word, they followed the high priestess into the main temple.

The ceremony was brief and simple, involving only the three of them. Other priestesses watched the ritual from a distance, but there was no reason for them to interfere.

Serafon added her personal blessing to the closing prayer, then dramatically spread her arms and commanded Zanos and Astra to rise from their kneeling position. A feeling of joyful disbelief touched Zanos as he hugged his wife and—

"Stop this ceremony!"

Vortius' voice rang through the temple like a mourning bell. The three at the altar looked around to see the gambler stalking toward them, closely followed by the same city magistrate and half a dozen guards.

"What is the meaning of this intrusion?" Serafon demanded with the full weight of her religious authority. Her hand settled lightly on Zanos' shoulder, and he knew she was signaling him to remain silent. Astra's powers must have warned her to do the same.

"Forgive us, High Priestess," the magistrate puffed as they approached the altar, "but this couple cannot be married. Zanos' gambling debts have lost him that right until he has made restitution. That is the law."

"And this is an old trick, Zanos!" Vortius exclaimed. "Trying to escape servitude by marrying a free citizen. Well, it won't work! Aventine law does not protect you in this instance—and certainly one of Morella's girls brings no dowry to—" His arrogant expression changed, his words trailing off as he stared at Astra's face. He seemed to be trying to place her, and looked greatly puzzled.

The magistrate, though, was only performing his duty. "Unless you have the money, here and now, Zanos, you must come with us to Debtor's Court, so that justice may be served."

Zanos wanted to laugh at his choice of words, but could only bring himself to show a contemptuous smile. It would be so simple to stop Vortius' heart—

Serafon's hand gripped his shoulder in warning, and the plea in Astra's eyes required no Reading power to understand. Zanos forced down his anger and wordlessly surrendered himself to the city guard. Let them think they had him; his powers would take him from whatever custody they locked him into, at the first chance to escape without detection. But Astra—

As they led him away, he tried something he had never done before. He projected his thoughts with the greatest intensity he could muster: *Astra, don't worry. I'll get away from them. Take the horses. When you reach the border station on the Road of Kings, I will be one day behind you. Do you understand?*

Astra nodded, her worried look easing. He smiled at his wife, then turned away to allow himself to be escorted out of the temple.

The four days that Astra spent on horseback, leading the two horses packed with the possessions she and Zanos shared, went by in a long gray blur. She slept in barns, stealing away before the farmers rose at dawn. Anticipation of being reunited with her husband buoyed her spirits, even though she could not detect his presence when she Read back behind her on the Road of Kings.

She camped about a mile from the border station, well off the road. A day passed. Another. And then a third.

Surely she couldn't have missed him! And he wouldn't go on without her. He wouldn't!

By the morning of the fourth day, she had become desperate enough to search for Zanos out of body. At last, she detected his presence—two miles away, on a different road, approaching a different border station.

He was part of a caravan of over two dozen people—a caravan led by Vortius. And as Astra Read them, she found most of them with the dull, blunted contentment of those locked in the grip of white lotus addiction.

And . . . Zanos was one of them!

Vortius now truly owned him, body and soul!

Chapter Five

The two-mile stretch of land between the roads was wild country, dotted with animal burrows that could break a horse's leg. Astra Read every foot of it, guiding her mount and the two packhorses across the treacherous ground. She was trying desperately to think of a way to rescue Zanos, but memories kept intruding—her conversation with Serafon after Zanos had been taken away—

"It was Zanos himself that Vortius wanted, wasn't it?" she had asked the priestess when they were alone in the anteroom. "We thought he was after his property!"

"So did I," Serafon had replied, "until now. I should have realized that this conflict was over honor, not wealth. Zanos defied Vortius. That could not be allowed. It was all I could do to keep Zanos from using his powers to kill Vortius."

"Why? The man was overwrought. If he had dropped dead of an apoplexy—" Astra looked sharply at Serafon. "You were protecting Vortius? It was Zanos who needed your help. I thought you and he were like mother and son!"

"They are both my sons," Serafon said quietly, sinking into a chair. "I am Vortius' natural mother."

Astra stared at her in disbelief.

"Thirty years ago," the priestess went on, "when I was a little younger than you, my Adept powers increased so that I lived in terror of being exposed. I'd never used my powers to harm anyone, only done what I could when someone was very ill or when the weather threatened to destroy our crops.

"A young boy in a nearby town showed Adept powers . . . and was stoned to death by his own family. I feared that the same thing might happen to me, so I decided to destroy my powers in the one sure way—by giving myself to a man. There was a neighbor it had been assumed I would marry—but he kept saying he couldn't afford a wife until the next good harvest. I was too frightened to wait, so I tempted him. It wasn't hard.

"My powers disappeared overnight . . . but the man lost all interest in me, and began courting another. Soon I discovered that I was pregnant. The father of my child had just announced his wedding plans.

"I feared the shame I would bring on my family. More than that, I questioned why the gods were putting me through one ordeal after another."

Astra touched her shoulder in sympathy. "So you ran away to Tiberium?"

"To this very temple. Many unwed mothers are helped here. When Vortius was born, the high priestess saw to it that he was adopted into a good family. Eventually I was allowed to join the order, and befriended his adopted mother. But I never told Vortius or his mother who I was."

Astra arrived at the border station a few minutes after Vortius and company had passed through the gate. She Read soldiers in the nearby barracks happily dividing up the bribe Vortius had given them to open the gates. The few coins she had would never satisfy their greed.

Three guards were on duty as she rode up to the tower. They looked down at her with leering smiles, exchanging muttered jokes that she could Read, but ignored. But it gave her an idea. . . .

"Hey, pretty one, what can we do for you?" one of the guards called down.

"Open the gates!" she demanded, not having to act to sound tired and frustrated. "He's not getting away from me that easily!"

The three looked at each other, puzzled, then back at Astra again.

"I've followed Vortius for two days!" she exclaimed. "The gold he paid you was supposed to include me. I'll chase him clear to the edge of the world before I'll let him desert me after what I did for him! Now let me through the gate!"

The guards started laughing, and Astra Read them envisioning this angry woman set loose on the arrogant gambler. As she had hoped, they resented his wealth enough to pass her through. She spurred her horse down the road, and rode fast until she was out of sight of the guard tower.

Then she slowed to a walk again. It would not do to catch up with Vortius' caravan until she had a plan to help Zanos escape. Again her memories intruded.

"Your powers returned after Vortius' birth?" she had asked Serafon.

The old woman had nodded. "By the time I joined the order they were as strong as ever. I found a new home here, and decided that I would have to find a better way to survive than running away again. Then I heard a Dark Moon Reader boast about exposing a secret Adept when he couldn't Read her surface thoughts. I could pass as a nonAdept if I could project my feelings, give Readers something to detect.

"Eventually, it became a habit to project my thoughts. And then I began to look for other secret Adepts, to help them survive in this land that kills us."

"Was Zanos the only one you found?" asked the Reader.

"Yes," Serafon said, smiling at the memory. "He was such a rebellious child. He escaped from his master and hid in the temple. Some instinct drew me to him, but I had to use my powers to prevent him from running away. I was amazed when he tried to counter my powers with his own weaker ones. I persuaded him that it was better for him to learn to control his powers than to reveal them while he was so young that he could be easily caught and killed. Eventually I was able to show him that the discreet use of his powers could be his way out of slavery, and we became friends."

Astra could Read a sense of apprehension sweeping the territory as she rode through the lands west of Zendi. Here and there she picked up thoughts of people preparing to join the army—an army marching against the Aventine invaders. These were the lands of the sorcerer Lenardo, she remembered. He and his savage friends would soon attack Astra's people . . . or defend themselves, depending on your perspective. Right now I, too, could be considered an enemy of the Aventine Empire.

She picked up images of Lenardo. His people saw him as a hero. They trusted him, and the union of Adepts and Readers he had brought together.

Constantly monitoring Vortius' progress, she Read that the gambler and his party avoided attracting attention. Astra did the same, skirting the places where people were gathering for battle. By evening, Vortius reached the foothills of a mountain range that stretched northward to the limits of her Reading abilities. There he made camp on a hilltop surrounded by dense forest.

The farther from the border she got, the more Astra worried about dangers she could not anticipate. Lenardo was a Master Reader. Scanning for enemies, he could accidentally discover her. I'll not be turned into one of the savages, as he was! But that meant rescuing Zanos that very night, so they could flee Lenardo's territory.

But how could she do it? Her only advantage was that she was a strong Reader, and there seemed to be no Readers in Vortius' party.

Yes, that was it! Serafon had unwittingly given her a clue. But she would need a place where she could imprison Zanos—and hold him.

She scanned the nearby hills. The area was dotted with underground caverns, but only one was structured to suit her needs. She made careful preparations, and with a prayer to all the gods set off toward Vortius' camp at twilight.

There were four guards on the camp's perimeter, each patrolling one quarter-section of the area. Zanos had the southeast quarter, standing like an armed statue, staring sightlessly into the darkness of the forest.

Astra crept to within a dozen yards of him, remaining behind the trees. Slowly and carefully she focused her mind on his, using a technique forbidden except under the strictest control in the healing of sick minds, salving her conscience with the thought that Zanos' drug-trapped mind was in desperate need of healing.

She projected an image, a belief into his consciousness—a picture of Serafon, weeping like a mother grieving over the death of her child.

Zanos drew his sword and moved in the direction he believed the "sound" came from. He stumbled into a clearing, looking for Serafon. Astra let the illusion fade, then stepped out from behind the trees.

"Zanos," she said softly, stretching out her arms to him, "come away with me!"

He stared at her, his blue eyes cold and empty. "Why should I go with you?"

The timing was all wrong; both the drug high and the period of suggestibility had worn off. But of course, Vortius would not send any man to patrol his camp in either of those conditions.

"I'm your wife," she tried. "Zanos, you have fought

for your freedom all your life. Are you going to let Vortius make you his property?"

The reminder of his lifelong determination made him frown for a moment, conflicting with the commands Vortius had implanted. Then Zanos shook his head. "I serve Vortius willingly. And you, my wife—you must serve him, too. Come. I will take you to him."

"No!" Astra took the hand he proffered, but tugged in the opposite direction—a futile gesture against the gladiator's size and strength. "Not yet, Zanos. Why . . . we've had no time alone together. Please—come with me to my campfire. Warm yourself, and be with me. I have your flute—don't you miss your music?"

"Music . . . yes. Our music will entertain Vortius," said Zanos.

It hurt her to hear him turn every suggestion to pleasing Vortius, but if that would get him to come with her, let him think what he chose. "Yes—we will get our instruments and practice."

"No—I must stand guard—"

"There are other guards," she insisted. "Vortius will be so pleased if you charm him with your music. Come, Zanos—he'll expect you to be in practice."

He stared at her coldly. "Astra," he said at last, as if he had finally remembered her name. "My wife. Yes, there are other guards, but I mustn't be gone long."

"Then just come with me to get the instruments," she begged. "It won't take long."

She led him through deepening night, Reading their way to the well-hidden cave where she had made camp. Far inside the hill, where none but a Reader dared penetrate the labyrinth of tunnels, she had prepared for her siege on Zanos' entrapped mind.

"We need a torch," he said.

"No—I can Read the way," she told him. "Just come along with me."

She had to win him tonight—if he grew desperate

enough to escape back to Vortius, dawn would reveal the rock chimney high above the campsite she had prepared. She had no doubt that a man of Zanos' strength, let alone Adept powers, could climb up and out. But the fire would not provide enough light for such a climb. She had until dawn.

When they came into the cavern, Zanos seized the flute avidly and played a few notes. The drug had not dulled his skill. No—it did not affect physical coordination.

Astra picked up her lute and accompanied Zanos, letting him lead the way. But he went nowhere except over the same old ground—the songs they always played, no variations, no improvisations, no syncopation . . . almost no style.

Finally, Astra undercut the melody with a new harmony, layering notes in an unfamiliar texture born of her fears and frustrations.

Zanos stopped playing. "What are you doing?"

"Don't you remember? You used to play like that, Zanos. You see what Vortius' drug has done to you?"

"It makes me strong."

"You are strong without the drug. Vortius has taken your freedom . . . and your music."

He didn't answer, but lifted the flute to his lips again, glaring at her as he played a variation on the same tune. But it was an old, well-rehearsed variation . . . and note by note Zanos slid out of it and back to the plain melody, accuracy without spirit.

Astra saw his eyes change—their blankness had disappeared with his anger, but now the anger dissolved to emptiness again. The notes fumbled to a stop. Zanos stared at the flute as if he had never seen it before.

Making no attempt to control her Reading, Astra watched him set the instrument down. "I have to go now," he said. "They'll miss me from the watch." He started to place his flute in its case.

"Zanos, you must clean your flute," said Astra, "or it won't play right next time."

"It won't play right *now*!" he protested. "I must go."

Was it hopeless? If he would not cooperate, she could not counter his strength—he could wander in the labyrinth of caves until he went mad with craving for the drug.

What good were all her plans to trap his body here, when Vortius had his mind trapped beyond her reach? Clea had begun her cleansing of the drug with the determination to be free of it. All she could Read from Zanos was an animal-like determination to return to his master.

But as she turned her eyes away from his empty ones, a thought suddenly reached her. //Astra! Don't turn away. Help me, Astra!//

Her eyes flew back to his, but the blankness remained. The thought had been weak, far away, and was not repeated . . . it was as if Zanos were trapped deep within his own mind, struggling for control.

"I will help you," she said.

"I don't need any help," he replied as if he had no idea that he had cried out to her. "Show me the way out."

"No."

"Show me the way, woman!" He towered over her, threatening.

But again she Read an entreaty from deep within him—no words this time, just a dim plea yearning toward her.

"Zanos, I cannot help you if you leave," she pleaded in turn.

"I don't need your help," he repeated.

"You do. You have lost your musical talent," she improvised hastily. "Vortius will be disappointed. I can show you how to play as well as you ever did."

He stared at the discarded flute. ". . . as well as ever?" he finally asked.

"Yes, Zanos!" Astra leaped at the opportunity. "Come—lie down. I will show you how to get your talent back."

"Lie down?" he asked suspiciously.

"You know how to go into healing sleep. You must do so . . . and let me guide you to regain your talent." She had none of the herbs used to put patients safely to sleep; if he would not willingly seek the healing trance, she could not reach his mind.

At that moment she longed for the Adept power to make him sleep . . . but her mind felt the weak but free Zanos within the drug-bound man exert every strength to prompt, "Heal . . . must be healed."

As if already in trance, he stretched out on the blanket beside the fire. Almost instantly he was in the dreamless sleep of healing—but no fever came to purge the drug from his blood. She would have to guide him to that.

To calm herself, Astra cleaned Zanos' flute and put it away, then settled herself carefully beside her husband. She would be leaving her body, not to observe a distant place or to seek a plane of privacy, but to enter the dangerous passageways of his drug-influenced mind. She swallowed hard, fighting down fear. She had practiced this technique at Gaeta, as all Readers did—but she was not a healer, nor had she colleagues here to draw her out should she become lost in Zanos' fantasies.

Long-practiced breathing exercises calmed her body, and she let her "self" drift forth. As always, her Reading became clearer than ever, unhampered by physical influences. She Read for Zanos—and found the part of his mind that refused the influence of the white lotus trapped, frustrated, within a body it no longer controlled.

//Astra!// She felt his shock as her presence touched his. Not a Reader, he had never experienced such a mental touch before.

//Yes, Zanos. I am here.//

//How can I hear you . . . Read you?//

She told him, //I am projecting to you. Now, I want you to leave your body, escape the influence of the white lotus.//

//Leave—?//

//Don't fear—I will guide you.//

She caught his natural reliance on his physical power vying with the loss of control since Vortius had drugged him. //No—your body won't obey you,// she prompted. //I will show you how to regain control.//

//I *know* how!// he replied in frustration. //But my own strength betrays me. *He* betrays me!//

//He?// Astra curbed her fear—the uniting of a fragmented mind was a task for the most skilled of Healers.

//Yes—he! Zanos the slave! Zanos the coward! He is the one in control begging Vortius to enslave him further.//

Suddenly Astra was engulfed in Zanos' memories. It was his day of triumph! The crowd roared as he skewered his third challenger and turned to receive their approbation, strutting before them, arms upraised, upon the sand stained with the blood of his opponents.

His heart sang. His master would win much gold on this match—and one-twelfth of it would go, as always, toward earning Zanos' freedom Ever closer the day grew—and now there would be more such bouts, with higher stakes—

A year—a year and a half at the most—and Zanos would have his freedom!

The cheering went on and on: "Za-nos! Za-nos! Za-nos!"

He circled the arena, basking in the approval of the crowd, long since inured to the knowledge that they would have cheered equally for his opponent had he been the victor, and Zanos a corpse to be dragged out of sight of the fastidious.

"Za-nos! Za-nos! Za-nos!"

He waved his arms, and the cheering increased as if he directed an orchestra. He reached the Emperor's box, stopped, saluted—the crowd went wild.

And suddenly fell silent as the Emperor rose. "Where is this man's master?" he called, and Lakus ran out into the arena to renewed cheering.

The Emperor raised his arms, and the people quieted once more. "Lakus, you have trained Zanos well—but he has gone far beyond mere training this day. I reward both of you for an outstanding display of gladiatorial skill. Lakus"—he tossed a small but heavy sack that clinked when Lakus caught it—"I reward you with three times Zanos' value. May you find another and train him just as well."

Then he fixed his stare on Zanos. "By Imperial decree, I declare you, Zanos, a free citizen of the Aventine Empire!"

The crowd went wild again . . . but Zanos felt his knees grow weak. It was all he had ever worked for, since Serafon had persuaded him his childish escape schemes were unworkable. He had his dream at last—and so unexpectedly!

His stomach hurt and his head swam as the people cheered the Emperor's generosity. Zanos knelt, bowing his head in a proper gesture of gratitude—but inside, he feared he might faint.

Zanos remained in that position as the Emperor and his retinue departed, and the crowd began to disperse. Then he climbed to his feet, wondering what had happened to the joy he was supposed to feel . . . and Lakus came over to him. "Congratulations, Zanos—and may the gods grant you good fortune. Be sure to put those arms away before you leave."

Leave? To go where?

His former master walked away, leaving Zanos in the rapidly emptying arena . . . a free man, but a man with nothing. Not even the armor he wore was his. He did not have a bed to sleep in tonight—nor a coin to buy supper.

This was the freedom he had longed for? To belong to no one? To have no one responsible for him?

Fear tore at his vitals as he faced the bitter truth: he was terrified of being free!

Astra could feel how sharply, even today, Zanos felt what he perceived as his cowardice that day in the arena. But it had not conquered him. //What did you do then, Zanos?//

//Oh—some young gamblers who had won heavily on me came to the arms room, and invited me to dinner. Before I went to them, I talked to Serafon—she arranged a room for me that night, and tried to make me see how happy I ought to be. The next day I went to my old master. By that time he was over his annoyance at the way the Emperor had taken his best man away prematurely, and was happy to hire me as a freedman. You know the rest.//

//Yes, I know the rest. Why do you castigate yourself years later for that one moment of shock? Zanos, *everyone* feels that way if his life suddenly, unexpectedly changes.//

//You don't understand,// he protested. //I felt *fear* of freedom—the same fear that holds me to Vortius now. Astra, a part of me yearns back to my days as a favored slave. After all, what did I have to do with my life except participate in the games, which I loved, keep my body in shape, and worry about nothing except the possibility that my Adept powers might be discovered? You have never been a slave, Astra. With a kind master, it can be a very . . . comfortable life.//

//But not for you. Zanos, I know you—//

//I thought I knew myself! But once that drug was in my blood . . . I saw my true nature. You will see it, Astra, unless you let me out of here before the latest dose wears off. I—this part of me that feels shame—I become weaker every day. Astra, I am not worth the danger you are in.//

//We are in the middle of the savage lands, Zanos. Where shall I go without you?//

//I don't know. I only know that I cannot help you.//

//Yes, you can. You have already recognized that it is a part *of you* that Vortius has trapped. Your mind is still whole. Come—let me show you how to leave your body. Then you will see everything clearly.//

But it was not that easy. Although Zanos was willing to integrate his personality, his depression was such that he could not leave his body. Astra understood—every young Reader faced such apprehensions, and Zanos was not a Reader at all. He feared that he would be completely disoriented, unable to return and regain control of his body.

//Do not fear,// she told him. //Read with me—*with* me, Zanos. Feel my love for you.//

//Let me hold you,// he responded.

//Yes,// she told him. //Yes—we will be able to hold one another once your body is free of the drug. But I cannot reach you now. You must reach out to me—//

She tried to guide his consciousness out and up, but he simply let her go. She returned, seeking his mind once more. //Zanos, I want you to imagine that you are not inside your head, but that you—the you that observes—are somewhere else.//

//I don't understand,// he replied.

The experience—not leaving the body, but observing from some perspective other than right behind one's eyes—was so common to a Reader that she could not imagine someone who had never done it. While Astra was searching for another way of explaining, Zanos said, //Do you mean preserving myself inside, as I do for a fight?// and suddenly his point of view was no longer from inside his head, but from somewhere inside his chest.

//That's it!// Astra told him. //Yes—that's right—now just follow me upward—//

She Read his surprise as his consciousness came out of his body. //Now free yourself,// she told him. //Do not feel your body anymore. Tired or rested, hungry or full, drugged or undrugged, it has no hold on your mind.//

For her, it had always felt like floating up and out of herself; for him, it was as if some heavy burden fell away when his mind became separate from his body. Utter freedom rang through his consciousness in joyous peals of laughter, and she joined in. //You have no fear of freedom, Zanos!//

//This is wonderful!// he replied. //Astra—where are you? I . . . I feel you, but I cannot see you.//

//There is nothing to see. You can see our bodies here in the cavern with us—//

//Why can't we forget them?// he asked. //Why can't we just stay like this?//

//Because if we do not return to our bodies they will die—and we will be left as disembodied ghosts, unable to find our way to where the dead belong. No living Reader has ever found the plane of the dead—and returned to tell the way. We have lives to live inside our bodies, Zanos. I have brought you away from yours only so that you may make a difficult decision—to rid your body of the drug Vortius has forced on you.//

//Yes,// he replied at once. //How did I fail to see it, Astra? All I have to do is use the healing fever—I've done it a hundred times to heal battle wounds. I can burn the effects of the drug out of my blood in a few hours!//

//Good. You understand what to do,// she told him. //But can you make yourself *want* to do it once you are back inside your body? The drug will control you again.//

//How?// he demanded in disbelief. //How can it? I am in control—//

//Now,// she reminded him. //Remember how you felt before you left your body—even when your body was unconscious, it affected you.//

She could feel him wanting to deny that, but she knew from experience what a difference there was between one's good intentions while free of one's body, and one's ability to fulfill them against the body's demands. //Plan every move, Zanos. Show me exactly what you are going to do.//

Again he found the skill from his gladiator's training: visualizing an opponent's every possible move and his own countermoves, feeling every muscle, every tendon doing its job until the difficult motions became second nature.

Now he tried to feel the way to start the healing fever—and found that he could not. //Astra, I cannot feel *anything*! Without my body, how can I?//

//But you do not feel those moves you plan with your body, Zanos. You feel them with your mind. Go on—show me how to counter an opponent coming at you with a spear.//

They were in the blazing light of the arena, the sun hot on their/his skin, waves of heat built from exertion rivaling the heat rising from the sand.

Opposite Zanos, a tall, slender but muscled man stood with spear at the ready. He drove straight at Zanos, who sidestepped and whipped his net under the man's feet with one deft move. A quick tug, and the man went down rolling, but by the time he swung his weapon around—

Zanos stood over him, not even breathing hard, trident poised to gut him.

//A spear is not a good choice of weapon for individual combat in the arena,//Zanos told Astra.

//That doesn't matter,// she replied. //What matters is that you felt your moves. Now, the same way, feel what it is like to start the healing fire through your body.//

That was more difficult; Zanos was not accustomed to visualizing his body at rest. //Wait—I know,// he said, and Astra was suddenly in pain.

It was a familiar pain to Zanos, the scrapes, strains,

bruises ignored during the excitement of a bout, which made themselves known as he cooled off afterward. //I wouldn't bother with healing fire for just that,// he told Astra, sensing her dismay. //It's nothing—just the way every gladiator feels after he's won.//

//I hate to think how they feel after they've lost!// she commented.

//Dead, most often,// he replied flatly. //The normal aches and pains ease with some herb tea and a hot bath. But I recall a time my arm was broken— one of the bones in my forearm, but I managed to hide it, for I couldn't let Lakus know I could heal a broken bone overnight.//

Astra felt with him the throbbing ache of the arm as he made his way back to his small slave's cell, collapsed onto his pallet, and called up the fire even as with his other hand he forced the bone ends together, adding Adept strength, but having to endure feeling what he did because he could not Read it.

As the heat of Adept healing surged through his arm, Zanos' pain faded. Probing the arm, he hoped he had set it properly—but he could not be certain until tomorrow. Carefully wedging the swollen arm between two cushions, he lay back and let the healing fire spread through his body as he fell into dreamless sleep.

//Yes!// Astra told him. //That is exactly what you must do! No matter how your body reacts, Zanos, you must set that same healing fire burning through it, until the drug is purged away. Is there . . . something that must be done to end the fire?//

//No. When all the foreign substance is cleansed from my blood, I will wake up . . . very hungry, but otherwise in perfect health.//

//Then . . . we must wait no longer. As you return to your body, be prepared for it to rebel.//

//I should be able to control for hours yet. The craving for the drug comes with the dawn.//

//Zanos . . . "look" at our cave.//

The first pale predawn gray was filtering down into the cavern, where the fire had burned to glowing embers.

//How long have we—?// Zanos broke off in astonishment.

//Several hours,// she told him. //Time has no meaning outside the body. It always feels strange to return. I will Read with you, help you to remain oriented. Perhaps you can keep from waking up—//

//But I *am* awake.//

//Your mind is awake. Your body sleeps. I wonder . . . Zanos, why don't you try to start the healing fire in your body before you reenter it?//

She Read with him as he concentrated on his own body below them, envisioned the warmth, fever, heat—

Nothing happened.

//It doesn't work,// he said. //I can't "feel"—imagining it isn't enough. There is something physical, Astra.// She Read him observe the growing light. //Stay with me—give me strength to resist the drug craving.//

//I will Read with you every moment,// she promised. //Now, imagine yourself lying just above your body, in the same position. Your body pulls you home . . . feel your breathing . . . your heartbeat—//

As Zanos sank back into his physical form, Astra Read the assault of the white lotus in his blood. A cold craving tugged at his mind, trying to force him to seek the substance to fill and warm that icy emptiness.

He denied it—but some part of him yearned for the easy pleasure the drug provided.

//Fight it, Zanos,// Astra pleaded. //Stay in the trance state, so you can Read me.//

//I can't—//

His breathing quickened, as did his heartbeat—if he came out of trance, she would no longer be able to project to him.

//The fire!// she told him. //Start the healing fire *now*, Zanos—cleanse the drug away!//

He was suddenly blank to her Reading.

Of course! The moment he prepared to use Adept power, he became unReadable!

With a roar of anger, Zanos woke, clambering to his feet. "Vortius!" he cried, stumbling out of the cavern into the tunnels, pushing Astra's body out of his way.

Astra had to let him go while she returned to her body. Because it had been moved, reorientation was difficult. The leaden weight of physical reality hung hard on her as she forced herself to her feet, ignoring bruises where one arm and leg had hit the rock surface.

"Zanos!" she called, letting her Reading range free.

He had gone down one passage in the dark, come to a turning, and was trying to decide which way to go. Groping with arms outstretched, he fell over a knee-high outcropping and sprawled full-length.

Enraged, Zanos bounded to his feet and turned, fumbling his way back to the light from the cavern. He ran to Astra, grasped her by the arms, and shook her. "You will show me the way out, woman!"

"No," she managed. "No, Zanos! Control yourself!"

He let go the bruising grip on her left arm, lifting his right hand in a threat to backhand her. "Show me!" he growled.

Determined not to be his means of returning to enslavement, she replied, "You may hit me—you may kill me, Zanos, but I will not show you how to get back to Vortius."

Something in her voice must have told him threats were useless. He let go of her right arm, too, and as she rubbed her tingling flesh he pleaded, "Astra— Read me. *Feel* what I need. If you love me, how can you do this to me?"

"How can you do this to yourself, Zanos? You have the means to escape that craving. Have you so soon forgotten what you decided during the night?"

"I can't," he said, sounding like a stubborn child.

"Of course you can," she told him. "You have overcome greater pain in the arena. You are brave, Zanos—and you don't have to suffer for long. Just until you set the healing fire burning through your blood."

"But I . . . I—"

She had to Read what he could not bring himself to say: he did not want to give up the pleasure the white lotus provided, glowing relief from care, relaxation of responsibility. It was easy to Read why the drug was so addictive—it took away all concerns, giving the momentary illusion of perfect freedom.

"Zanos—what the white lotus is doing to you *now*—is that freedom?"

". . . no." But it was a reluctant admission.

"Then free yourself. Clea did it, without your powers to help her. Ignore your pain, Zanos—it's less than you suffered from a broken arm. Lie down, and call up the healing fire to purge your blood—"

Her hypnotic tones lulled him, and like an automaton he knelt once more, lay down—and saw the sky above the cavern.

"No, Zanos!" Astra cried as once again he jumped to his feet, his blood yearning toward the source of fulfillment.

As she had feared, the climb was not difficult for a man in Zanos' prime condition. She tried to follow, tearing her hands and bruising her knees and ankles on the rocks—but Zanos was tough and calloused, levering himself easily upward toward the light— toward the freedom which was slavery—toward Vortius!

Chapter Six

Hopelessly, Astra clung to the rock face high above the campfire, out of breath, her limbs aching with the exertion. She could not concentrate in her despair, and so her Reading was wide open, Zanos' growing hunger for the white lotus turning her insides into a sucking vacuum, screaming to be filled.

"Zanos—wait!" she cried without knowing what she said. "Don't leave me! Take me with you to Vortius—I will take the white lotus with you."

He stopped, peering down at her, silhouetted against the growing light. Then he held one huge hand out to her. "Yes, Astra—yes, my love, come with me."

Unthinking, she scrambled toward him, breath burning in her lungs, arms trembling. She reached for an outcropping, clung to it with her left arm as with her right hand she reached toward Zanos. Her toes lost their purchase, throwing all her weight onto her left arm—which had no strength left.

Zanos' hand grabbed for hers, missed—

Despite all her volition, her left arm shook uncontrollably. Her elbow straightened and her hand began to slip—

Suddenly, her body was moving without her will, her thrashing right arm captured as if in Zanos' net and wrapped around the outcropping of rock. She clung in terror, her face against the rock, blood pounding in her ears as she Read the cavern below. It sucked her downward just as the craving in Zanos sucked at him, at them—

"Climb down," Zanos said. "I will help you, but I cannot lift your whole weight with Adept power."

"I can't," she sobbed, knowing she held on by his will, not her own. She closed herself off to Reading with all her strength, enclosed in a physical world of touch and sound, her eyes squeezed tight as if to shut out the knowledge that she could not remain there, had to do *something*.

"You must move," Zanos told her. "Astra, I won't let you fall—but you have to climb down yourself!"

He climbed down toward her, but there was no ledge at that level wide enough to allow him to pull her to him. "Go on," he insisted. "Reach down with your left foot . . . Astra—*Read*, for Hesta's sake! Find the hand- and foot-holds. I promise—I won't let you fall."

But she was paralyzed, her head burning with fever, her hands and feet numb with cold. She couldn't get her breath . . . until she allowed herself to Read Zanos beside her, ignoring the growing pain in his own body out of his concern for her.

He came back to me!

Leaning emotionally on his strength, she found the courage to Read for a lower foothold, to let go the false safety of the rocky outcropping and grope her way downward, holding her Reading very carefully to her immediate area, lest she be sucked down into that whirlpool again. Each time her physical strength failed, Zanos would blank out of her Reading. Astra felt panic when that happened, but then his Adept strength would hold her, strengthening her trembling limbs until—

Zanos let go! As he fell past her, Astra screamed— and fell—

Into his arms.

He had dropped only a short distance to the cavern floor. Astra, concentrating on her Reading, hadn't realized they were almost down.

Zanos hugged her tightly, whispering, "You're all right! Astra, I'll never let you be hurt—please, don't cry. You're safe now."

But her tears came from her realization. "*You* are all right, Zanos! Oh, my husband, you've come back to me!"

He set her on her feet, very carefully, as if she might break. Then he stared at her, blinking, the agonizing cramps ripping through his body at total odds with the joy he felt as he said, "Yes! Astra—you mean more to me than any drug!"

And then he doubled over with the pain.

Astra dropped to her knees beside him, Reading chills shaking him even as sweat beaded his skin. "Zanos—"

"No—" he gasped. "It's all right now. Just pain—" He gritted his teeth as a spasm convulsed him. "I know—what to do—about pain."

He sank down again on the blankets, and this time when his presence disappeared to her Reading, Astra felt the healing fire begin in his chest, spreading outward—a raging fire burning worse than the agonizing cramps. Zanos' face was a mask of pain as he endured long enough to be sure the fire would continue. At last, he let himself sleep.

"Thank Hesta," sighed Astra, sinking down next to him. Her trembling slacked off as she realized the nightmare was over. They were out of the Aventine Empire, and now they were free of Vortius—

Or were they? The gambler would certainly have his men out looking for Zanos by now, and he had to have hours of healing sleep before they could leave. Astra would have to protect him.

How could she do that? She had no strength, no courage. . . .

But looking at Zanos, who had overcome his drug craving for her sake, she decided, *I must ignore my fear, as Zanos ignored his pain for me, and do what has to be done.*

Apprehensively, Astra let her Reading power stretch beyond the cave, searching for their enemies.

Zanos woke to a world of light and shadow. He squinted as he sat up, for the noon sun shone almost directly down the rock chimney.

"Astra?"

There was no answer. A part of him wanted to believe that his returning memories were nothing but a bad dream, but everything he saw confirmed the truth: Astra had risked everything to free him from Vortius and the white lotus. His feelings of love and gratitude, though, were soured by anxiety. Where *was* she?

He climbed slowly to his feet, weak and very hungry. He needed more sleep—but it was hunger that had wakened him. There was probably some food among the supplies Astra had brought, but he couldn't think of that until he was sure she was safe.

He heard hoofbeats outside. Was that Astra returning? What if it was someone else?

He couldn't get out through the labyrinth—only a Reader could find the way. After a time he heard footsteps—but there were also renegade Readers in the savage lands.

His back flattened against the cave wall, Zanos braced his meager strength and waited. In moments, Astra came through the entry—and jumped when she saw him.

"Don't *do* that!" she breathed. "I thought you'd still be asleep."

His only reply was to grasp her and kiss her, needing the warm reality of her in his arms. She dropped the small sack she was carrying, and at the smell of sun-warmed berries the needs of his body overwhelmed the needs of his heart, and he released her.

"You frightened me," he said. "I was afraid Vortius' men had captured you."

"They could have captured both of us," Astra said as she sat down by the smoldering fire. "I took the horses and set up a false trail—I hope I did it right. I tried to make it look as if we headed back toward the empire."

"Good thinking," he said, sitting down next to her. "That will buy us a little more time." Ravenous, he tore open the sack and began devouring berries.

Astra gave him an understanding smile. "I'm sorry I couldn't bring you back some meat. I don't know how to hunt or trap—and besides, I can't cook. The Academies hire cooks. Students just serve the meals and clean up afterward."

"I can cook," he told her. "I had to learn after I gained my freedom. It was a long time before I could afford to pay for meals, and nutrition is important to a gladiator. Don't worry—I'll teach you to cook. And to use a sword."

"A sword? Me?" She laughed at first, then must have seen or Read that he was serious, for she added, "I don't know a thing about fighting."

"The best reason for you to start learning at once. Astra, we don't know what we'll face between here and Madura. The more combat skills we have between us, the better. I packed extra weapons among our supplies."

"I noticed," she said. "Very heavy. Zanos . . . I don't know if I'm *capable* of hurting another person. I saw how helpless you were this morning, and if I had to I would try to defend you. But I hope I don't ever have to!"

"So do I, but we cannot count on that much good fortune, as far as we have to travel."

"Where do we go from here?" she asked, changing the subject.

"North," he said, finishing a spring apple and still feeling ravenous. "First we get at least a day's ride away from Vortius, to gain time to plan. Right now, my powers are too weak to risk a confrontation with him and his men."

"You won't have to confront him. You're free of him now."

"Yes, thanks to you," he acknowledged. "But what he did cannot go unanswered. He enslaved me and my gladiators with white lotus, and further degraded us by giving us two overseers—Ard and Lanna."

"So he got them to betray you," Astra concluded, "by giving them power over their former master."

Zanos nodded. "Call it regaining honor or call it seeking revenge, I will see them again before we reach our goal. And this time there will be no Aventine law to protect them!"

"But how did Vortius force you to take the white lotus? With all your Adept powers—"

"—I'm no Reader," he replied ruefully. "Nor am I as powerful an Adept as you think. I can't do most of the things the savage sorcerers do. I can't even change the weather, as Serafon can. And no amount of Adept power can protect a nonReader from a cowardly blow to the back of the head. By the time I regained consciousness, wine laced with white lotus had already been poured down my throat . . . and my mind was no longer my own."

He cringed at the humiliating memory, but forced himself to continue. "They tied me up and took me to a dark room somewhere. Vortius fed more of the stuff to me, until I believed anything he told me." He spat out a piece of apple core in disgust. "If not for Serafon, I'd have killed him long ago. I should have!"

"I understand," Astra said quietly. "That's why Serafon never told you that Vortius is her son."

In stunned silence, Zanos listened as Astra told him things Serafon had never told him in all the years he had known her. When she finished, he managed to ask, "Vortius doesn't know?"

"No. I don't think she could bring herself to—" Astra stopped suddenly, her eyes focused on something beyond the cave wall.

"What's wrong?" Zanos asked. "Vortius?"

"His men are riding this way again. My false trail didn't fool them. They're perhaps a quarter-hour away—"

"Then let's go!" Zanos snatched up the blankets and musical instruments, and they quickly repacked everything. Astra led the way out through the caverns. They fastened their supplies to the packhorses and climbed aboard the other two mounts.

"I know how to avoid them," Astra said.

"Then you lead the way," Zanos said, grabbing up the packhorses' reins.

The trail Astra chose took them well east of Vortius' camp, but Zanos felt as if he had missed a confrontation with his enemy by a hand's span. And even though the men searching for him were far behind, he could not shake off the feeling that they were being closely pursued.

"We're safe now," Astra announced as she slowed her horse to a walk. "They've turned back to their camp."

"Vortius is afraid of the hill bandits," Zanos told her. "That's why he needed so many men—large bands of robbers in these hills. Another reason you must learn to defend yourself."

"I've already agreed," Astra replied. "I just don't know if I can learn it."

The next few miles passed in silence. Astra seemed to be concentrating more than she had been back there when Vortius' men were following them. He wondered if it was an act, to avoid discussing the lessons she didn't want to learn. *But if she doesn't learn to defend herself, what will happen to her if we're separated—or if I'm killed?* After all, male Readers were trained in swordplay, so it couldn't be true that a Reader couldn't stand to harm another person.

But she was a woman—and his wife. This business of being a husband carried responsibilities he hadn't fully considered when they were back in Tiberium. *I think I'm starting to understand what Serafon meant.*

When they stopped to rest, Zanos used his Adept powers to kill a rabbit, then started a cooking fire to roast it. While he was skinning and gutting it, Astra went foraging again—and only when she returned and he saw her eyes skitter away from the sight of the roasting rabbit did he remember that Readers kept to a vegetarian diet to preserve their powers.

But she shared what she had found, berries and mushrooms and greens. Nonetheless, Zanos noticed that she kept her face turned away from him as he devoured the meat his body craved.

Eventually Zanos broke the tense silence. "Are you going to be uncomfortable every time I eat meat?"

She managed a hesitant smile. "No. I know you need it. I'll learn to prepare it for you—Zanos, I *understand* that you have to eat such food for both your physical strength and your Adept powers."

"And I can see why you hadn't even the strength to lift your own body out of that cave back there. Astra, that's not a balanced diet."

"No, it's not," she agreed. "But it will be if I can get some cheese and nuts and good bread. There must be places where we can buy—"

Suddenly her eyes widened, and she gasped. "A Reader! Zanos—there's a Reader only a few miles from here—and he's broadcasting a warning to other Readers!"

With Zanos standing guard, Astra left her body to Read what was happening on the seacoast. The Aventine fleet was attempting to enter the natural harbor on the west coast of the savage lands. On a hill overlooking the harbor she found the source of the mental voice: a young male Reader was just returning to his body, which lay on a spread cloak. Nearby two men stood facing the sea, both unReadable.

"They refuse to turn back, Wulfston," the Reader said as he sat up. "They think their army is too big to be defeated."

The older of the other two—a young black man with the bearing of a leader—frowned angrily. "I expected as much. Let them know that we are about to give them a demonstration."

The Reader lay down again on his cloak, and did not even bother to close his eyes before leaving his body. *He's blind!* Astra realized. This had to be the renegade Torio, whom the savages had raised from the dead!

Astra Read him move among the shiploads of soldiers, sailors, and Readers, "heard" him broadcast another warning, telling them that their ships would never reach shore. Back on the hilltop, the black man put a hand on the arm of his other companion, a frail-looking youth who was also blind. "Ready, Rolf?"

"Yes, my lord," the boy replied, and both of them became unReadable once again as a strong wind suddenly rose, shaking the Aventine vessels to and fro. Astra watched their sorcerers' powers in action with horrified fascination. Only two people trying to stop that vast flotilla—and she felt they actually might succeed!

The "demonstration" ended with no damage to the ships or their occupants.

Torio pleaded with the Aventine Readers to make

the fleet reverse course, but the invaders refused to turn and run from two Adepts and a renegade Reader.

It was after sundown when the first ship neared the shore, ready to unload troops and Readers. But the two Adepts conjured up another windstorm out of the cloudless sky, much fiercer than the first. Ships whirled like toys—one capsized, breaking apart and spilling people into the churning waters.

Astra watched helplessly as at least a dozen people drowned—six of them Readers. Their mental screams clawed at her like the screams of those who had died at Gaeta.

Zanos put more wood on the fire to keep off the evening chill, then carefully placed a blanket over Astra's still body. Every few minutes he checked to be sure she still breathed.

His mind went back to the ordeal they had shared in the cave, both in and out of their bodies. It seemed like much more than one day had gone by since then, while this waiting for Astra to return felt like an eternity.

I should be with her, he told himself. If he could do that Reader's trick while he was under the influence of the drug, surely he could do it easily now that he was back in control of himself.

But someone had to remain here, guarding Astra's body in this strange forest while her spirit performed a Reader's prime function: to search out truth. And after watching the care she had taken before leaving her body—looking for a smooth and level patch of ground, spreading a blanket on the spot, and then gingerly positioning her body on it—he knew that there was more to this trick than he had thought. There was so much he could learn from her, perhaps as much as he wanted to teach her about—

A soft moan signified Astra's return. Zanos dropped

to one knee beside her as she sat up, obviously upset. "Are you all right?" he asked. "What happened?"

"We're in more danger than we thought," the Reader replied, and told him what she had just witnessed. "These Adepts may not really be able to turn ships to stone, but their methods are just as effective."

"Wait," said Zanos, settling beside her. "There's something you said that I don't understand. This Torio warned the Aventine Readers three times to turn back? And the Adepts gave them a demonstration of their power and a chance to retreat?"

"Yes, but—"

"Astra, if I had that much Adept power, and an army invading my lands, I might bother with one warning before defending myself—but certainly not three! And the storm. You said it destroyed only three ships? What about the others?"

"They managed to get away," Astra replied.

"When the Adepts ran out of energy? They couldn't sink all the ships?"

". . . no," Astra admitted. "I had the impression that they could have kept the storm going for some time, but—" She stared at him. "Zanos, are you defending the savages?"

"No," he replied. "I'm just sharing my feelings that there is something wrong—something unexpected here. You said the three savages told the survivors of the shipwrecks to come ashore?"

"Yes, and the Reader broadcast a promise that they wouldn't be harmed. He was wasting his time, though. No Reader would risk it, and none of the other survivors could Read his message."

"What about you?" Zanos pressed. "Did *you* believe his message? Was he sincere in wanting them to come ashore?"

"Well, of course he was—think what they could do

with a dozen more Readers, their minds twisted like Torio's to work against their own people!"

Zanos nodded, but asked, "Did anyone else go ashore?"

"Yes," Astra admitted reluctantly. "There were people from Lord Wulfston's lands to help soldiers and sailors get ashore. What do you make of all this, Zanos?"

"When someone invades your land with an army," he explained, "do you waste manpower and resources taking any prisoners but valuable hostages? The commanders of the army would make bargaining tools—but from what I know of military tactics, the commanders approach the shore only *after* the land has been secured. So all this 'Lord Wulfston' has got is foot soldiers and seamen to feed and house—a cadre of his enemies inside his own land. That sounds incredibly foolish to me."

"Maybe he plans to turn them all into loyal savages," Astra suggested. "Twist their minds against the empire."

"Three shiploads of people?" he reminded her. "That's at least sixty people, probably more. Even supposing this sorcerer has that much power, he hasn't got the *time*. That fleet will find a place to land and march into his territory from another direction. Wulfston will have to meet the invaders and protect his people—or his own subjects will turn against him."

Astra shook her head in confusion. "Why would he rescue Aventine citizens from a storm he created? He could have drowned them all. Zanos, you can't suggest it was out of the goodness of his heart. Wulfston and Torio were the Reader/Adept pair who devastated the hospital at Gaeta!"

She was right—anyone capable of such an act would not be motivated by humanitarian principles. "I don't know," he replied. "But there's more to these savages than we thought, Astra. We certainly can't assume we understand them!"

The next morning, Vortius broke camp and continued north. Zanos and Astra did the same, using hill trails that paralleled the gambler's course, but always kept them out of his sight. In recovering from his ordeal with the white lotus, Zanos had remembered that ten of the caravan's packhorses carried nothing but sacks of gold, a fortune to rival the Emperor's treasure house.

"That gold represents misery and death, all caused by Vortius," he told Astra. "Before I kill him, I have to find out what he plans to do with it, why so many had to suffer for his greed."

Zanos was unReadable, waiting for Astra to offer to try to Read Vortius' plans. She refused to take the cue, reluctant to take part in his vengeance. *I'm afraid again, but why fight if we don't have to, and for no good reason?*

When the caravan stopped to rest and feed the horses, so did Zanos and Astra. And that was when Zanos insisted on beginning his wife's lessons in swordsmanship.

The short sword he gave her might have been light by *his* standards, but she found it unwieldy. And Zanos was a harsh taskmaster, insisting that she repeat the primary exercises until her shoulders ached and her palm was blistered—and although she put her best efforts into following his instructions, he soon lost patience.

"Astra, you're not even trying!"

"Yes, I am!" she cried, throwing the sword away from her in disgust. "Zanos, I'm not a fighter! I can barely lift that thing, let alone make all those fancy moves."

The gladiator took several deep breaths, obviously bringing his temper under control. "I'm sorry," he said softly. "It may seem I'm asking too much of you, but I know I'm not. You may not be a swordswoman, but you are a fighter. You fought the corruption in the Readers' system—"

"No, I didn't," she said on a stab of shame. "Tressa wanted to fight it, but I was too frightened. I fought Portia only when she attacked first—she *forced* me to defend myself."

"And we may meet attackers who will force you to do much worse," Zanos stated matter-of-factly. He picked up the sword and wiped the blade clean. "Here." He replaced it on the belt too large for Astra's slim frame. "That's enough practice for the moment, but I want you to keep wearing it."

"Keep tripping over it, you mean!"

"You'll learn to move with it. Come on—Vortius will be moving soon."

They covered several miles of hill trails without exchanging a word. Astra's powers monitored Vortius' party without her having to concentrate on the task, leaving her conscious mind free to think about what she had left behind. Tiberium might have become too dangerous for her to stay there, but it had been home, and she missed it. She remembered teaching music to the young girls at the Academy, ignoring her current aches and pains by remembering—

Smoke!

She was jolted out of reverie by the sight and smell of a thick black cloud on the northwest horizon. Far too big to be a campfire.

"Zanos—"

"I see it," he said, pulling up next to her. "Can you Read that far?"

It was about two miles away. "By the gods!" Astra breathed. "It's a village being raided!"

"Vortius?"

"No. I don't know who—"

Three score of men were setting fire to the wooden huts of people who could barely fight back. She saw a young girl carried off by an ugly brute who laughed at her terrified screams.

An adolescent boy snatched up a sword and ran at the man, only to be cut down from behind by another raider, who laughed, "Gotta share her now, Yorgo!"

Astra screamed at the boy's death agony, and withdrew into herself, separating her mind from the pain.

Zanos touched her shoulder.

"I'm all right," she said tersely. "But those people are being slaughtered!"

The gladiator looked to the east, then back at the smoke column. His indecision lasted only for a moment. "Come on!" he said, kicking his horse to a gallop.

Astra slapped her horse's flank and took off after Zanos, the sword slapping against her thigh.

They rode into a scene of devastation. Bodies littered the ground, the cries of the dying mingled with the crackle of flames. Astra Read a handful of survivors as she and Zanos dismounted.

"Which one first?" he asked, eyeing the bleeding bodies.

Astra ran to the side of a girl of about twelve. She lay unconscious, a large gash in her right side. Even with her limited medical training, Astra could tell that no Aventine healer could stop that bleeding—but . . . "Zanos—?"

He knelt beside her, placing his hands over the wound. The bleeding stopped almost immediately, and the girl drifted from unconsciousness to healing sleep as her severed flesh drew together.

As Astra began Reading other survivors, Zanos suddenly exclaimed, "This one!"

She whirled at the intensity of his voice, to find him kneeling over a leather-garbed man who writhed in pain. Her husband gripped the man's upper right arm in anger, not concern.

"He's one of the raiders, Zanos, not—"

"I know that! Read him for me!"

Startled at his tone and manner, Astra nonetheless complied. "Internal bleeding, and severed tendons in his upper calves." She guided Zanos in stopping the bleeding and reconnecting the tendons, but in the midst of it their patient suddenly passed out.

"There," Zanos said with satisfaction. "He'll stay unconscious until I can question him."

"Question him about what?" Astra wanted to know.

"Later. Right now there are his victims to help."

With Astra's guidance, Zanos used his healing powers on two other severely injured villagers, then asked, "Are there any others in danger of death?"

"No, but—"

"Good." But as he turned back toward the unconscious raider he coughed. Their eyes watered in the acrid smoke. "Maybe some of their homes can be salvaged," said Zanos—and where he looked, the flames died away, revealing that several dwellings might be made habitable.

But Astra saw that Zanos' efforts were depleting his strength. "Please," she told him, "use your powers for healing." There were still an old woman with a skull fracture and concussion, and a young man with a broken collarbone. Zanos worked on them while Astra Read the others—but when he joined her at the side of an unconscious middle-aged woman, he staggered against her, breathing heavily, close to exhaustion.

Just then a scream from behind them caused both Reader and Adept to turn. From the other side of the village came a young woman, hair loose and disheveled, shrieking an attack cry as she charged them with a sword.

The moment of surprise brought Astra's Reading wide open. She could sense the girl's frenzy and Zanos' weakness in the same moment.

Instinctively, Astra jumped to her feet and stepped in front of Zanos—

Within five paces of Astra, the girl suddenly seemed to trip and fall. She landed at the Reader's feet, unconscious.

With a sigh of relief, Astra turned to thank her husband, who was sinking back on his haunches, barely able to stay awake—

And only then did she realize that she had drawn her sword, and was gripping the hilt tightly with both hands.

Zanos woke to find himself lying on a straw mat in one of the huts he'd saved from the flames. Astra sat tailor-fashion not far from him, cleaning her sword with an oil-soaked rag.

"Good morning," she said as he sat up. "How are you feeling?"

He almost replied, "You're the Reader—you tell me," but remembered that they were in a land where Aventine Readers were feared and killed. Looking around warily, he asked, "Did I pass out? The last thing I recall was . . . stopping someone from attacking you."

"You expended all your energy saving the villagers, putting out the fires, and then saving me—again," she told him. "You hadn't had time to recover completely from the white lotus, either. But you didn't pass out; you went into a kind of trance. After I straightened things out with Trel, we got you into this hut, where you fell asleep."

"Trel?"

"He's sort of the village elder. He and Kimma—the woman with the sword—were returning home when they saw the smoke, just as we did. When they arrived and saw the destruction, Kimma assumed the strangers she saw here were responsible. That's why she attacked. But when Trel saw you put her to sleep rather than kill her, he wasn't so quick to assume we were his enemies."

"But how could you communicate?" asked Zanos. "You don't speak their language—"

"No, she doesn't," said a voice from the doorway, "but I still speak Aventine."

Zanos looked past Astra to the gray-bearded man entering the hut with a tray of food. This had to be Trel, a tall, thin man of more than sixty years, but with the stride and bearing of a younger man. His most striking feature was clear blue eyes. They seemed to take in everything, revealing little. The eyes of a hunter.

"In fact," Trel continued, "everyone in the village speaks at least a little." He gestured Zanos to remain seated, handed him the tray, and sank to a sitting position. Smiling, he held out his hand. "I welcome you to my home, friend Zanos, and thank you for what you did yesterday."

Zanos and Trel grasped one another's forearms as a sign of newfound friendship. It was a long time since Zanos had done this with sincerity . . . not since he had befriended Ard. He pushed away that memory as their host bade them eat.

"One of the people you saved is Deela, my wife," Trel added. "Astra told me when she Read Deela this morning—"

Zanos stared at Astra in astonishment.

She said calmly, "No, I didn't tell them I'm a Reader. I didn't have to."

Trel chuckled. "You missed the sight of your wife holding me at bay with her sword. The moment she spoke, I knew she was Aventine, and well educated. But she doesn't have the arrogance of the highborn. She was more than a little surprised when I assumed she was a Dark Moon Reader."

"And when did you escape from the empire?" Zanos asked.

Trel's smile faded. "I didn't. Thirty-five years ago,

this area was part of the Aventine Empire. My family had a small farm in the lowlands. Then Drakonius pushed the border back a few miles—right over our land. We and some of our neighbors fled into the hills, and survived by staying out of Drakonius' way. Our village had a Reader, which made it much easier for us.

"Eventually we settled here, fighting off the roving bandits until our rights were respected. Then we found we could trade with them."

"You never tried to get back into the empire?" Astra asked.

The old man snorted. "From what I've heard, the present Emperor is no better than the one who ruled when our lands were lost. If there was justice in the empire, would you two have run away? Here, we enjoy a good measure of freedom . . . or we did until recently." He continued sadly, "Many of the clans call these the Red Hills, for all the blood that's been shed in them. Robberies, raids—not to mention feuds between clans. Our village was always the calm within the storm—until yesterday. We've paid a severe price for becoming lax and overconfident. Yesterday morning we were nearly fifty. Now we are fewer than twenty."

"But who attacked you?" asked Zanos. "And why?"

"The clan of the White Crow," Trel said tightly. "Of all the bandit clans, they're the most vicious and cowardly. They usually camp southwest of here, robbing people on the trade routes between the lands of the Black Wolf and the Red Dragon. But when the Aventines invaded the lands of the Black Wolf two days ago, the Crows took flight—raiding any settlement in their path. It was bad enough that they took the food we worked so hard to store, but to kill and destroy, just for sport—"

"Perhaps because of envy," Astra said. "Success draws many jealous enemies. That's a harsh lesson my husband and I recently learned."

Zanos said, "We'll find out what their motives were when we question the prisoner. Is he still unconscious?"

"No, but he's not going anywhere," the old man replied. "I bound him hand and foot before he woke up. He's been doing a lot of cursing. Why did you save his life? Do you know him?"

"Not exactly," Zanos replied. "I recognized the sunburst tattoo on his arm. The last time I saw it was over twenty years ago—on the arm of every crew-member of the *Sunrider,* the slaver ship that took me to the Aventine Empire!"

Zanos cut the ropes that bound the prisoner, then backed away toward the tree stump where Astra was sitting. Except for these three, the village center was deserted. The raider stared at them warily as he rubbed circulation back into his limbs. But he couldn't get up.

"We stopped the bleeding and closed your wound," Zanos said as he sheathed his knife, "but I didn't heal the nerve damage in your legs—so you can forget about running away. We'll finish healing you after you've answered our questions. I am Zanos, and this is Astra, my wife. What's your name?"

The man said nothing, staring defiantly.

Zanos let out an exasperated breath. "Astra?"

"His name is Sarno," she said flatly, and terror leaped into the hill bandit's eyes.

"Yes, she's a Reader," Zanos said. "She could pull every thought, every secret out of your mind, but we'd rather you tell us freely. I don't want to hurt you, even though I have plenty of reason. You are a former slaver, and I . . . am a former slave."

Sarno's reaction was a laugh full of bitterness and anger. "Aye," he replied, "I was a slaver. For less than a year."

"Aboard the *Sunrider?*" Zanos prompted.

"Aye." Sarno slapped at the tattoo on his arm. "I

signed on an' took 'er mark, then found I was in a dyin' business—a slaver on a route where slaves were becomin' hard to get and even harder to sell. They need lots o' slaves in an empire that's growin', not one that's havin' its borders pushed back ever' few years. And there ain't many kingdoms buys slaves anymore, not in this part o' the world, anyhow."

"And the *Sunrider* got its slaves from the northern islands, right?" the Maduran pressed.

"Wrong," Sarno threw back. "Hadn't fer years afore I signed on. Somethin' happened in them islands . . . tales the old crewmen whispered about when they got drunk. Bunch o' nonsense, sounded like t' me."

"What kind of tales?" Zanos demanded. "Tell me!"

"Only one that made any sense," the slaver said. "Another slaver ship, the *Hawkwing*, was the last one t' take slaves out o' Madura. And the crew didn't take 'em on in chains—they run aboard, glad t' get away, no matter how!"

"Refugees?" Astra questioned. "What were they fleeing?"

"Don't know. Whatever it was, it killed every crewman who had any kind of Adept powers, 'cep the captain—an' he went mad, they say. The survivors landed on the western shore somewheres, and fell in with the hill people. That was about four years ago. Some o' me shipmates an' me left the *Sunrider* last year, after business dried up an' smugglin' had too much competition—"

"Zanos—duck!"

Even as Astra tried to knock him aside, Zanos instinctively dropped and sheltered her with his body. Two arrows whistled over them—one of them thunking sickeningly into human flesh. Sarno screamed once and slumped, the arrow through his heart. Scrambling behind the inadequate shelter of the treestump, Zanos looked toward where the arrows had originated.

"There!" Astra pointed. "Up in the trees!"

Yes! About fifty paces away. With a wave of his hand, Zanos set the trees aflame. The two archers yelled in fear as they leaped from their hiding place. Even before they hit the ground, the Adept was on his feet, concentrating his powers. The killers' hearts stopped.

He concentrated again to extinguish the fires, just as Astra warned, "Behind you!"

Zanos spun and leaped aside as a ball of fire came hurtling at where he had been. The Adept who threw it was standing openly at the north edge of the village, pressing his attack with more fireballs. Zanos stood his ground and deflected them, then tried to stop the hill bandit's heart. The other Adept clutched at his chest, but resisted—just as Zanos had done in his last arena battle. They were locked in a struggle of powers and wills when—

"Zanos!"

He heard Astra's cry, heard other bandits attacking, *felt* Trel and Kimma rushing into the fray, swords swinging.

But he dared not move, couldn't let his concentration slip or the other Adept would win out and kill them all.

He kept up the pressure, knowing they were evenly matched, knowing that only determination would decide the winner—until finally his opponent screamed and dropped to his knees.

But Zanos dared not collapse in relief—it could be a ruse to make him let down his guard.

And as, indeed, the bandit glanced in his direction to see where to direct another Adept blow, Zanos reached out once more with his full powers—and the man collapsed, dead.

Breathing heavily, he turned to look for Astra— and found a world of silence. The battle was over. Several bandits lay dead. Trel and Kimma were unhurt, looking grimly satisfied, while Astra—

Astra stood by the tree stump, unmoving, staring

at nothing. Her dress was covered with blood, as were her hands—and the blade of Zanos' knife. He didn't even know when she had taken it from him.

Slowly, her fingers loosened their grip and the knife fell. Zanos ran to her as she tried to sit down on the stump, stumbling over the corpse of the man she'd killed.

Zanos grabbed up his wife and held her gently in his arms. "It's all right, Astra," he whispered. "It's all right. . . ."

But *she* was not all right. Her skin gray with shock, she suddenly clutched him with incredible strength, and screamed.

And screamed. And screamed.

Chapter Seven

" 'First kill'?" Trel echoed.

"It's the term used in gladiatorial training," Zanos explained. "Some react to the experience without remorse. Others work it out with their consciences, as I did. And still others"—from his sitting position, he glanced over his shoulder into the hut where his wife lay sleeping—"experience deep trauma, like Astra."

"I see." The old man nodded. "Most of us here go through the experience, sooner or later. Kill or be killed is the natural law of this land."

"I know. Astra had to understand that. I just wish she hadn't learned it this way. I had to put her into recovery sleep to stop her hysterics, but she's the one who knows how to help injured minds, not me."

"Perhaps the rest will be enough," Kimma said gently. "That . . . and your love."

"I hope so, because that's all I've got." He sighed. "Mowart! If only I could've stayed at her side, to protect her!"

"What you did protected us all," the woman reminded him. "I was closest to Astra when the one with the sword came at her—but there were two others after me. I could see her dodging that sword—I guess her Reader's powers let her evade his moves. Finally she pulled off her cloak and threw it in his face. And then she saw your knife—"

"I don't even remember her taking it!"

"She had to," said Trel. "She was unarmed—hadn't touched her sword since she cleaned it this morning."

Zanos sighed. "I have to make her wear it. She says it's too heavy—and after today, she may never pick it up again."

"She will," Trel assured him. "If she's only half the woman I perceived last night, when she helped us prepare that mass grave, then she will be everything you need in a wife. Only a woman of the strongest character would be willing to travel with you all the way to Madura."

Zanos looked up sharply. "How did you know that?"

"From the way you questioned your prisoner. We stayed out of sight, as you asked, but we had to know what you wanted with him. We overheard every word, and . . ." Trel paused to look at Kimma, then back. "Friend Zanos, we'd like to ask you to delay your journey. These are dangerous times for all of us. The hill clans fear that the Aventines will retake these lands. They're like animals before a forest fire, not knowing which way to run, attacking anything in their path. We need your help to keep those of us left alive."

"It might be better if you moved your village on north," Zanos observed. "Your wife and the others will be well enough to travel in a few days."

"This is our homeland," the old man said firmly. "We've fought long and hard to keep it. Besides, from what Astra told us last night about Lord Wulfston and the Aventine fleet, I don't think their army will get very far inland.

"But it's more than not believing the Aventines can defeat the new alliance. I've been waiting thirty-five years to see the end of Drakonius' reign, and something better rising up to take its place. That finally seems to be happening. The Adepts and Readers who now hold this cluster of lands base their rule on peace and trust rather than the terror and oppression with which Drakonius ruled."

"If it's such a good alliance"—all three of them started as Astra stepped out of the darkness of the hut—"then why aren't you a part of it?"

Zanos jumped to his feet. "Astra—"

"I'm all right, Zanos," she said flatly, her upraised hand stopping him from touching her.

"But you were asleep for only an hour or two."

"You put me into recovery sleep. I've recovered."

Have you? he thought as he scrutinized her. She had the sleepy look of someone needing more rest, but her entire attitude had changed. She was . . . cold. Could her first kill have changed her that much?

She turned to the village elder. "I would like to know why you have not joined this wonderful alliance, Trel."

"I'm a cautious man, and a very patient one," he said slowly. "An alliance is like a young tree: it must survive a few storms before it's able to bear fruit. This alliance weathered an attack by Drakonius and his allies two years ago, and an attempted takeover by several strong Adepts last year. Now the Aventines are challenging them, this time with a powerful army. I believe the alliance will successfully defend us all, and eventually make a peace treaty with the empire. The prophecy will come true."

"Prophecy?" Astra questioned.

" 'In the days of the white wolf and the red dragon, there shall be peace throughout the world,' " he quoted. "The lands just east of here belong to Lord Lenardo, whose symbol is the red dragon. Bordering his lands to the east are those of Lady Aradia, whose symbol is the white wolf. Their marriage last year became the heart of the alliance, and the center of all our hopes. When the young tree has grown a bit more, I wish to taste of its fruit."

"You may find it bitter," Astra said grimly. "Last

winter, two members of this alliance destroyed the largest hospital in the Aventine Empire—with an earthquake. A *hospital*, Trel, full of sick and injured people. Hardly an act to promote peace."

"I hadn't heard that tale," Trel replied with a frown. "Who saw them actually start the quake?"

"Portia, the Master of Masters."

"Is she someone whose word you can trust?"

A strange look crossed Astra's face. ". . . no," she finally admitted.

"I do not want to speak ill of the Master of Masters," Trel said gently, "but she must be very old by now—Portia was Master of Masters when this was still part of the empire! Can you be sure she told you the truth? As I recall, she's related to the royal family some way. Could it be that a natural earthquake destroyed the hospital, and the members of the alliance were blamed to give the Emperor support in this war?"

Astra nodded mutely, and Zanos sympathized with her confusion. What if these savage rulers were not mad brutes, as they were portrayed in the empire? But on the other hand, what reason did they have to trust them?

"I suppose that's possible," he said. "But if Lenardo fled Portia, how does that prove he's more to be trusted than she is? It could be that she wouldn't allow him the power he wanted in the empire, so he found it among the savages. I think you are right to wait and see how well these new rulers govern before you throw your lot in with them, Trel. As for Astra and me, we're moving on. You are welcome to join us."

Astra stared at Zanos, wide-eyed. Then suddenly she got up, and walked back into the hut without a word.

Trel and Kimma looked at one another, and left with vague words about looking in on the injured.

Zanos followed Astra into the hut, where he found her tuning her lute.

Some instinct warned Zanos not to unpack his flute and join her—she was in some kind of very personal mood, shutting him out more effectively than if she had barred a door against him.

So he just sat down on the mat, listening to Astra play her "thinking song," as she called it. All the beautiful chords were there—but her spirit was missing.

Finally, he reached over and put his hand on the strings of her lute, stopping the music. She looked at him with questioning eyes.

"You have to *tell* me what's bothering you," he said softly. "I can't Read you, Astra."

"I'm waiting for you to tell me what other decisions you've made," she replied without expression. "When we move on, how long you'll let us stay here, what we'll do about Vortius—"

"I don't understand."

She pulled the lute free of his hand. "I thought I was supposed to share your life. For the past two days, all I've been is your personal Reader! 'Read this for me!' 'Scan over there!' 'Monitor Vortius—!' "

"I had to make decisions for our survival."

"Our survival doesn't depend on killing Vortius. It depends on our making a sensible plan. Except for your wanting to avenge yourself on Vortius, we *have* no plans."

"That's not true," he said. "We plan to go to Madura. Or at least I thought we did. You don't really want to go, do you?"

"Yes, I do! Returning to your homeland is important to you. But do we have to rush right out of one dangerous situation into another?"

"We don't know that it's dangerous to go to Madura."

"After two warnings? Two warnings that some 'great evil' is killing Adepts in your homeland, and you still want to rush into the unknown. You'd prepare for weeks for a single bout in the arena, but you won't make any preparations for this. Why?"

"If you are too frightened to come with me," he said bleakly, "just say so."

"Yes, I'm scared!" she shouted, shoving the lute aside with no care for its delicacy. "If you weren't so stubborn, you'd admit that you're frightened, too! You want to keep chasing after Vortius so you don't have to stop and think about the dangers ahead of us. Zanos, you've not even recovered from the white lotus yet. We've had one ordeal after another since the day of the games, and we need a *rest*. At least Trel and his people accept us. Can't we stay, even for a little while? Long enough to figure out what to do next?"

"I know what I'm going to do next," he stated firmly. "I'm going to find Vortius and kill him. Even if you want no part of it, that is one thing I *must* do, Astra."

"Zanos—" Her face twisted, and he searched the depths of her eyes, trying to understand, desperately wishing he could Read the emotions he could see but not interpret. She suddenly shook her head. "We don't know each other at all! How could we—we don't even know ourselves!"

"What do you mean?"

Astra stood up and retrieved her sword, hefting the heavy weapon with both hands. "You told me to wear this until 'something happened.' Well, it happened yesterday. First Kimma attacked us, and then Trel confronted me. Right then, I was *glad* to have this thing, even if I'd have made a very poor showing." Zanos saw her eyes change again, this time showing the cold anger he sometimes saw in a deadly opponent in the arena. "And when that bandit attacked me today," she went on bitterly, "I needed this sword—I was sorry I wasn't wearing it! When I saw your knife within reach, I thanked the gods . . . but after I used it—"

Zanos stood and placed his hands around hers as she tightly gripped the hilt of the sword.

She looked up at him then, and her anger faded. "I didn't scream because I'd killed that man," she said, hardly above a whisper. "It was that I realized . . . I was glad I'd done it! I *enjoyed* killing him, Zanos! Is that what you want me to be—a killing machine, like you?"

"Astra," he pleaded, trying to pry the sword loose from her hands, but she wouldn't relinquish it.

"Is this what I have to be to survive in your world?" she asked, transferring the sword to one hand, and putting her other arm around him. "Then I'll become a warrior for you, Zanos. I'll learn the way of the sword, my husband."

The next day, the last of the survivors came out of healing sleep. The village showed its gratitude to Zanos and Astra with gifts and the offer of one of the huts for as long as they wanted to stay. A cheer went up when the Reader and the Adept accepted.

Early that afternoon, a man rode into the Settlement carrying the young girl Astra had seen being carried off by the raiders two days before. She had suffered at the hands of her captors, but Astra could read her joy at returning home.

Deela and Kimma helped the girl down from the horse and into one of the huts, while Trel greeted the rescuer and introduced him to Zanos and Astra.

"Without their help, Javik, there would have been no Settlement for you to bring Seela back to," Trel told him.

Javik—a balding man of about fifty but with the bearing of a fighter—gave the couple a curt smile as he thanked them. "Let's sit down and break bread," he said. "There is much I have to tell you.

"The war is over," Javik explained, "and the Aventines lost. Badly."

Astra swallowed hard, almost afraid to ask. "How many died?"

"Less than two score . . . on both sides."

Trel stared at him. "Forty people? Out of two armies numbering thousands? How can that be?"

"After the ships were stopped at Dragon's Mouth, they sailed south and set the army ashore to march northward by land. The people of the Black Wolf met the first of them in a brief conventional battle. That's where the deaths occurred. Then Wulfston, his Reader, and perhaps a dozen of his minor Adepts arrived on the battlefield. The area was a wide, sandy plain. The Adepts surrounded the Aventines, then used their powers to trap the army in quicksand."

"Quicksand?" Astra repeated. "How could they do that?"

"Quicksand is just sand and water," Zanos told her. "Wulfston's Adepts probably broke through a dam and let the plain be flooded."

"Oh, no—they kept it completely in control," Javik said. "They made it rain on the enemy, then moved pools of rainwater wherever they wanted them. The Aventines lost their supplies and weapons, and a lot of the troops sank into the mire, but not one of them was allowed to drown. But they were helpless—no choice but to surrender. And Wulfston not only let them live . . . he fed them, and then told them to go home!"

Astra was astounded. "A handful of people defeat the largest army in military history—then just tell them to go home? Javik, are you certain?"

The older man, who had given the impression of a person with no special powers since he entered the village, was suddenly open to Reading. "I Read it for myself, Astra. What the watchers are reporting is true."

"You're the Reader who helped Trel's people survive Drakonius' takeover," Astra identified.

"I was just a boy, new to the Path of the Dark Moon then."

"Aye, but we'd not have survived without you," Trel put in. "But go on. What else has happened? Has the Aventine army agreed to go home with their tails between their legs?"

"What else could they do? Wulfston did take hostages—two Master Readers. I couldn't Read his intentions, but I have a feeling that it has something to do with negotiating a peace treaty. If the Emperor doesn't agree, he's a fool. His whole army was taken by just *one* Lord Adept. And their alliance is made up of *four* of them."

"Yes," agreed Trel, "the watchers reported that Lenardo and Aradia left for the land of the Black Wolf. I take it they arrived too late for the battle."

"Aye," replied Javik. "They sent a message to Lady Lilith to return home—but that went north of here."

"Watchers?" Astra questioned. "What do you mean? There aren't supposed to be Readers among the savages, nor have I sensed any."

"Not Reading, sunwriting," Trel explained. "The watchers relay messages and news by flashing codes with mirrors. At night, they use lanterns. Kimma and I were out reading their messages when the White Crows attacked here."

"If I'd been here to warn you—" Javik said grimly.

"You're only one man," said Trel. "We had to know what was happening in the invasion. Thank the gods you found Seela."

"The hill clans are on the move all over this area. It was chance that I ran across the ones holding Seela—you left fewer than half of them alive, and most of those still licking their wounds. By the time I ran into them, they'd had a clash with another clan and had little interest in tangling with *me*."

Astra studied the man's whipcord body—with that

strength and Reading powers combined, he must indeed be a fearsome object to the local clans.

"A second clan attacked us yesterday," Trel told him. "They're all going insane!"

"Not without reason," Javik replied. "You know how the clans are—cowards and bullies, but independent. There's someone trying to unite them—someone who's had considerable success with the newcomers."

"Newcomers?" asked Zanos.

"Since the alliance defeated Drakonius, the clans have been swollen with former slavers and troops from his defeated army—people used to working together as a team. A lot of them dream of capturing lands for themselves. If they could form their own alliance and attack just one Lord Adept at a time, they might succeed."

"No," said Trel, "not against *these* lords. That was what those four Adepts tried only last year, when they attacked Lady Aradia. She escaped to Zendi, and the rest of the alliance rallied immediately to the defense as a unit. It was the attackers who lost their lives."

"Yes—but what if they had kept her separate—attacked when the others could not come to the rescue of a single member? That seems to be what Seriak plans."

"Who?" asked Trel.

"A new bandit leader. He's only a minor Adept, but he's wily. He's already gathered over a hundred men around him, and they've taken an area in the hills up in the land of the Blue Lion, either killing or absorbing the hill bandits. The Lady Lilith may be their intended target. Her castle is far from the lands of her allies—but of course she has her own retainers, and her son Ivorn is said to be developing rapidly into a Lord Adept in his own right. I doubt Seriak would try until he has more Adept talents in league with him—but he is someone we must watch."

Astra agreed. "Can you tell me where he is?"

"I'll show you—you are a Magister Reader, are you not?"

"Yes," she admitted.

"I thought so. I wouldn't dare go so far out of body alone, but you won't get disoriented."

"Wait," she said. "You can go out of body? You said you were put on the Path of the Dark Moon when you were just a boy."

"And deserved it," he replied. "But a man learns to do what he has to—and to save my people I had to make my small abilities stretch. I Read best out of body—but I dare not go far, and I've never tried to reach another plane for fear I couldn't find my way back."

"You are very brave," she said. "I cannot imagine any Reader trying to learn such a thing alone. When you are rested, we will travel together to where this Seriak is, and find out what he is plotting."

While Javik slept after his long journey, Zanos proceeded with Astra's lessons in swordsmanship. Trel had found a light sword she could wield without straining her arms, and Zanos began teaching her to use it, trying to remember when he had been an adolescent boy just beginning his training as a gladiator, before he had developed the strength of maturity.

But a woman was built differently from a boy. Astra did very well in the school exercises, but once they exchanged real swords for wooden weapons in a practice match, he found that Astra's arms were too weak to allow her to deflect more than a few blows before he could simply beat her sword down with sheer strength.

"That's not fair!" Astra protested, panting.

"Of course it's not fair!" Zanos told her. "Do you think some hill bandit is going to treat you with courtesy? Astra, use your advantage—I'm not using Adept power. Can't you Read what I'm going to do and counter it?"

Astra tried—he could see that she did know what he was about to do—but her responses were too slow. "You're thinking about it," he told her. "Don't think—act. Think with your body, not your brain!"

Still she was too slow. He struck her time after time, raising welts on her arms and legs—and when he stabbed at her chest, instead of parrying his thrust she stepped back, trying to shield herself.

"Astra!" he said in annoyance. "You're wearing enough padding to stop a *real* sword!"

"It still hurts!" she insisted.

"Of course it does," Kimma suddenly spoke up. She had been watching them for some time now. "Zanos, have you ever tried to train a woman to fight before?"

"No—of course not," he replied.

"Well, we've got different instincts from men," she told him, "because our anatomy is different."

"I've noticed," he said wryly.

"No—you haven't," insisted Kimma. "Every time you strike Astra's chest padding, it bruises her breasts—and a woman's instinct is to protect them. Astra, may I borrow that sword?"

"With pleasure," Astra replied.

"Let me show you how to take advantage of a man's instincts," she said. "Remember—we are definitely not bound here by any rules of fair play."

Intrigued, Zanos faced off against Kimma. She was about the same size as Astra, but had the strength brought on by her life-style. Still, she was certainly no match for him in muscle power. So . . . she didn't try to be. She stayed on the move, darting in and out, making him twist and turn to keep up with her.

"Woman may not have men's strength," said Kimma, "but we have endurance. Zanos is arena-trained—I probably can't wear him down this way, but I could most ordinary men."

Zanos agreed. "A valuable lesson, Kimma. Thank you."

But the lesson wasn't over. Suddenly Kimma ceased dancing about, and began to strike at Zanos as if she were trying to finish off a tiring opponent. But he was not tired. Easily, he deflected blow after blow until—

Kimma struck high, as if slashing at Zanos' throat. As he lifted his sword to counter her, she suddenly swung wide and came in under his guard—straight toward his vitals!

The pain, the horror of the day he had been wounded there, was on him in a flash of terrified memory—he lowered his sword instinctively to protect his manhood—

And Kimma's sword sruck him so hard in the center of his chest that despite the padding he was knocked back a pace, stumbled over the tree stump, and landed on his backside with bruising force.

In utter disbelief, he just sat staring up at the woman who—had the fight been real—would have just killed the undefeated champion of the Aventine Empire!

Kimma looked over to where Zanos' wife stood watching in wide-eyed astonishment. "And that, Astra, is how a woman gets a man to drop his guard."

Blind male instinct rushed through Zanos—he wanted to grab Kimma and strangle her!

But a gladiator who survived was one who learned his lessons with good grace. He felt the hot flush of his skin turn from fury to embarrassment—could almost feel his wife Reading him for fear that something besides his pride had been wounded.

Suddenly it was as if he could see the scene from outside himself, the ridiculous figure he cut, sitting there helpless before the savage swordswoman—

And he burst out laughing. "Kimma," he said as he climbed to his feet, "I said we can't count on our opponents fighting fair—but you've reminded me of what that really means!"

Astra came to him and touched his arm—as if

Reading were not enough to reassure her that he was all right. Then she turned to Kimma. "You don't understand—Zanos was once actually wounded that way. His reaction—"

"No, Astra," he assured her. "Any man would react the same way. It is pure instinct—and the move is one no man would use against another, knowing what it would provoke. When Sporius wounded me, it wasn't deliberate. He meant to disembowel me, but I made a misstep dodging his blow and— Never mind. I don't want to remember.

"But my point is this: the threat of permanent damage is quite different from a knee to the groin in street fighting. That traditional low blow is so painful that the recipient often passes out—but there is no permanent damage. You threaten a man with a knife or sword, though, and you rouse his most primitive response.

"I killed Sporius. Accident or no, he had dealt an illegal blow and the match was mine—but I could not think. I merely reacted. He had dropped his guard in horror at what he had done. I had my sword in my hand, but I dropped it—and I broke his neck with my bare hands before the officials could reach us to stop the match. Only after that did I pass out."

Astra was staring at him. Kimma said, "Astra, what your husband is saying is that if you use this technique to make your opponent drop his guard, you *must kill* him. Otherwise, he *will* kill you." She turned to Zanos, swallowing hard. "My apologies. I knew you had the discipline of a gladiator, and so trusted you to react as you did, since of course I didn't actually touch you. If I had known of your injury, though, I would never—" She blushed crimson. "Oh, Zanos—I am so sorry!"

"It's all right, Kimma," he replied. "*I'm* all right. The woman who trained me to use my Adept powers was able to heal me."

"Oh." And Kimma's blush deepened even further.

Astra broke the embarrassed silence. "Show me how to do what you were doing earlier, Kimma. You were leading Zanos a merry chase that would wear down any man but a gladiator."

From that point on the lesson went better. Astra began to discover her own advantages—and when Kimma left them to their practice once again, Zanos found his wife's reaction times much improved. When he praised her, she replied, "I finally realized how to do it when Kimma was choreographing steps for me almost like a dance. It's like music, Zanos—we don't stop and think about what notes to play. We just play them. What you said—the body, not the brain. I know it's going to take long practice—but at least I've got the feeling for it now."

But she was worn out; no use to ask more of her today. It would take time to build her endurance— but how much time did they have?

That evening when they retired to their hut, Zanos examined the welts on Astra's arms and legs, some of them turning into nasty bruises. He placed his hand over the worst of them. "I'll—"

"Don't," said Astra. "The bruises are nothing—and you must save your strength."

"Taking care of you is what my strength is for," he replied, and let the healing power flow through the worst of her bruises.

"Thank you," she whispered, snuggling up against him like a sleepy child. But she wasn't a child—she was his wife. "Kimma said your breasts were bruised," he said, laying his hand over her left breast through the soft cloth of her gown. "We'll see if we can't rearrange the padding tomorrow—maybe Kimma can find something more cushiony."

His hand could not be still, but gently pressed her breast, feeling the nipple respond. So did his own body, and without thinking, he bent to kiss her mouth.

Tired, Astra remained passive for a moment, but

then her own feelings woke and she put her arms around him. Instantly, he was aflame with postponed desire as Astra cuddled against him.

But when he pulled back and began to lift her gown away from her body, she suddenly pulled it out of his hands, saying, "No, Zanos! You know we can't!"

"Then why—? What did you think we were doing?"

In the dim light he could see only surprise on her face. "I thought—it just feels so good to touch each other—"

He groaned, awareness of her total innocence making her seem more a stranger than on the day they had met. "Astra—now *you* must learn a lesson in anatomy. A man can't be satisfied with just touching—at least not that way. I love you, and you arouse desires we dare not fulfill."

"I'm sorry!" she whispered, and pulled away. "Oh, I wish we were somewhere safe—that I didn't have to Read to the castle of the Blue Lion tomorrow—that you didn't have to preserve your powers lest we be attacked. Zanos . . . how long is it going to be like this? All the way to Madura? Are we never going to dare to express our love?"

The next day, Astra asked Javik, "Have you ever been married?"

"No." He studied her. "I never dared."

"I thought you said you had been placed on the Path of the Dark Moon. The Masters arrange marriages for all such Readers—to ensure the next generation for the Academies."

"I'm sure they would have," he replied. "I was only fifteen when they failed me, though—too young for the responsibilities of marriage. I was assigned to Trel's village as assistant to their Reader, who was over seventy years old then. He didn't survive Drakonius' takeover—but I did, and had to learn to Read then as best I could to keep my people safe.

"Sometimes I've thought about the future—about

who will Read for the Settlement after I'm gone. But every time I decide I should marry and have children, hoping that at least some of them will be Readers, some new danger crops up, and I need every bit of my meager powers to protect us." He smiled sadly. "I suppose I'm still not too old—but I'm so accustomed to relying on my powers that even if the world were to become a safer place, I'm not sure I could bring myself to risk losing them."

"Are you sure you would?"

"Nothing is sure," Javik replied. "I know that most Readers' powers return after they've been married for a while. Or at least return in part. Unless *that's* a myth, too! So much of what we were taught in the Academies has turned out to be false—but I left so young that now I'm not sure what we were really taught, and what was just gossip circulated among the boys. I take it you are asking because you and Zanos have not yet . . . ?"

"That's right. And what do you know about Adepts?"

"The same, so far as I know—which only makes sense." But then he suddenly became UnReadable for a moment, saying, "Let me show you where Seriak's encampment is, near Lady Lilith's castle. It will be a pleasure Reading with a Magister—it's many years since I've worked directly with another Reader."

They lay down on the mats in Zanos and Astra's hut, Zanos standing guard over them, Trel and Kimma outside. When they left their bodies, Astra felt that uncertainty in Javik she had sometimes felt in the students at the Academy who were just learning to do this—fear that once out of body, they would not be able to return.

But Javik's presence reached out to hers and became steady and secure. Then he led northward, following landmarks instead of using the technique Astra would have used had she ever visited Lilith's castle before—simply imagining the place and suddenly being "there."

However, it was still only minutes before they "saw" the castle, a huge structure sitting on a steep mountainside. Something about it implied great age and benevolent wisdom.

Javik led her to the hills beyond—where there were signs of a deserted camp, but no people. //Seriak was camped here just a few days ago.//

//But he's gone now,// Astra told him, Reading in every direction without locating any large groups of people except in villages. //The Lady Lilith has returned home—perhaps he's afraid to stay so near an Adept. As long as we're here, let's have a look at that castle.//

Within the castle, Astra Read—

She withdrew quickly, Javik following her without question.

//Readers! Two of them, Javik!//

//Yes—I Read them, too. This is where Lord Wulfston sent his two hostages, Amicus and Corus. How far can Master Readers travel out of body, Astra? Could they communicate with Tiberium?//

//No—that must be why they brought them here. I'm going to try to Read them more closely. Don't communicate with me, or they'll Read our presence.//

//Just lead—I'll follow.//

The two Master Readers were not in the dungeon, as Astra would have expected, but languishing in lavish guest quarters on the second level. Both men appeared to be in good health, well fed, and comfortably attired. Only the locked doors with guards stationed outside gave evidence that the two Masters were prisoners and not guests.

Master Amicus was staring out one of the narrow windows, openly thinking about the homeland now lost to him forever, an invitation for Master Corus to communicate, Astra understood—but a possible danger to her if he caught her eavesdropping. But there was too much information to be gathered for her to withdraw.

The savages wanted Amicus and Corus to see the peaceful intentions of the alliance, and eventually persuade the Emperor to consider a peace treaty.

What they didn't know was how the Aventine Readers feared the savage sorcerers' mind-twisting powers. They would never trust the word of Readers who had been the prisoners of the Lords Adept. Even if the empire eventually conquered the savages and he and Corus were released, their own people now regarded them as dead men. What did the future hold, then? He had been forced to swear on his Reader's Oath that he would not take his own life—but could a dead man be bound by an oath?

Astra empathized with the man's sense of isolation—made especially piquant by the presence of another Master Reader in the next room, firmly closed to Reading. Amicus was offering an apology—but Corus refused to listen.

By the simple expedient of waiting for his thoughts to turn to it, she found out how Amicus had wronged Corus when they were captured by the savages. Amicus and Corus, out of fear, had done nothing about their suspicions—even knowledge—of Portia's corruption. When Lenardo had been prying for what they knew, Corus might have confessed—except that Amicus had attacked him—had actually grappled mind to mind as Portia had with Astra! No wonder the other man was unforgiving.

I wish he had confessed. I wish I had. They probably would have killed us, but—

Astra Read Amicus' heartfelt wishes that he could undo all the wrong decisions he had ever made—and most of all, that he could make it up with Corus and once more be friends, fellow Readers. It was hard to be sympathetic, though, with someone who wished he had taken a different path only because of where the one he had chosen had ultimately led.

Corus remained steadfastly closed to Reading—Astra guessed that he would never trust Amicus again.

Then her errant powers picked up a surface thought from Corus—something very peculiar. Not Reading, he was not sending his thoughts out clearly the way Amicus was—she wished the other Reader would stop trying to get through so she could Read—

Corus was *glad* that he would not be returning to the empire! He felt . . . safe? There was a phrase running through his mind, like a talisman: "When the moon devours the sun, the earth will devour Tiberium."

"A prophecy?" Zanos asked when Astra told him what she and Javik had learned.

"It sounds like one—but from so long ago that the prophet who spoke it is long forgotten. Lenardo and his friends believe it—and believe that it will happen soon. Lady Lilith is preparing to join with the other alliance members in some plan to avert disaster."

"The earth will devour Tiberium," Zanos mused. "That has to mean another earthquake. Are you sure they don't plan to *cause* one? There's a solar eclipse due sometime soon."

"About Summer Festival," said Astra. "That would fulfill the part about the moon devouring the sun, all right. Zanos, I can't Read Lilith at all—she has full Adept powers. I found her by visualizing, and she was directing her retainers to prepare for her absence. She *told* them she was needed to help prevent a disaster. Of course, she could have been lying."

"So could Serafon," Zanos said suddenly. "She's not too old to have come with us—look at Trel! I think she knew that prophecy, too, and stayed behind to use her own powers to help avert disaster, or to save people if it happens."

"So either she will be working alone against the force of the savages and nature," Astra said, "or she will soon have plenty of help. The members of the savage alliance plan to take every minor Adept and the few Readers they have and sneak into the empire."

Every day Astra and Javik Read both to Zendi and back to Lilith's castle. There was no sign of Seriak— apparently he had tired of waiting and gone elsewhere to plot for power. To Astra's relief, there was also no sign of Vortius. If Zanos became involved in the fate of the Settlement, perhaps he would eventually grow beyond his need for revenge.

Everything they could Read pointed to the savage alliance's sincerity in trying to prevent disaster in Tiberium. Some among them knew Aventine Readers on the Path of the Dark Moon—and brought about an uneasy treaty to get the network of Readers they needed for their project.

"I wish we could join them!" said Javik. "I've come to believe they intend only to help."

But when the Lady Lilith left her castle, riding straight south to meet with Wulfston, Lenardo, and Aradia near where they would enter the empire, Zanos wondered, "Why are they leaving now? Summer Festival is twenty days away."

"I don't know," Astra admitted. "They're following Lord Lenardo—that's all I've been able to make out."

Trel was apprehensive. "It's all very fine for those strong Adepts and Readers to go try to save the Aventine Empire—but who's going to look out for their lands while they're gone?"

The idea, it seemed, was for potential enemies not to know they were gone. The watchers sent their messages as usual: hill clan movements, weather warnings, trade caravans. But never a word about the movements of the Lords Adept.

Each day Astra and Javik Read out of body, finding life proceeding in Zendi, in Wulfston's castle, and in Lilith's just as if the rulers were at home. But while in the southern lands people saw their rulers seldom, at Lilith's castle there were no crowds for the Lady Adept and her son to walk concealed among . . . and the local peasants began to wonder why they were never seen.

One day as Astra and Javik were about to withdraw from their surveillance, Astra felt Master Amicus' sudden startlement.

Carefully, she Read with him. He was Reading northward, to the deserted outlaw camp. It was still empty, but below it, on the road leading to the castle, rode a dozen men.

Strangers, the watcher on the hillside flashed to the one on the castle tower. *Merchants, by the look of them*.

But Amicus could Read the real threat, miles away, just outside Lilith's border: a small army, perhaps two hundred strong. Certainly enough to take the castle, provided the Adepts were away!

Astra Read the Master Reader's indecision—should he call for the guard and give warning? Would he be believed? Besides—he was being held prisoner here. Why aid his enemies? If that army attacked before Lilith returned, what hope had the people around here of defending the castle?

But the invaders were pure savages—if they won, and then found out he was a Reader, they would certainly kill him. Those so-called merchants were scouts for the distant army. He could Read what they discovered, follow them back to their camp, assess their chances—

If it appeared they would win, he would pose as a nonReader and throw in his lot with them while he decided whether to sell them his skills or make his escape. But if Lilith returned before the attack, then he would give the warning, and try to make a powerful friend in the Lady Adept.

Amicus' self-serving meditations sickened Astra, and she withdrew from his mind lest her feelings give her away to him. The group of men posing as merchants approached the castle and hailed the watch. "Fine goods to offer the lord or lady of this excellent household!" cried their leader—and as he did so, the thought occurred to the two watchmen that their lady had been remiss in rewarding them lately—they deserved the silver coins the man held out, glistening in the sunlight.

"A small reward for your service, men—get me an audience with the ruler of this land, and you will be rewarded further." And again, images formed in the men's minds, of golden coins, of silk for their wives—and of Lilith denying them, taxing them, taking their lands. All lies—but for that one moment, they believed that their mistress had wronged them, and deserved to lose their loyalty.

"The Lady Lilith be not here, sir," one of them replied.

Not to be outdone, the other said, "No, nor her son neither—but mayhap ol' Rondivore will trade wi' ye. Come in, come in, gentlemen—"

And they led the party inside, where they could look over the plan of the castle, plot their attack.

"Hey! Orfo! Mulbur! Don't let those people in!" another guard on one of the towers shouted down to the watchmen. "You know our orders—"

And as he reached for his horn to blow a warning, his breath caught in his throat. He choked, gasped for air—but something blocked his windpipe! Face purpling, he fell to his knees, other men in Lilith's livery running to aid him, pounding him on the back as he coughed and choked.

And Astra realized that a man among the merchants who had looked casually up at the tower was unReadable except physically. The "leader" looked toward him, and he shook his head, obviously not wanting to be noticed as he slipped something to the other man.

"Aye, Seriak," murmured the ostensible leader, and called, "Ho there—here's a potion will help that poor fellow!"

It was not the drugged potion, though, that captured Astra's attention, nor the way the guardsman's choking fit ceased the moment it was forced between his teeth. No—she was Reading the face of the man they called Seriak, a face which, although now bearded, was burned into her memory so that she would never forget it: the face of Vortius!

Chapter Eight

"So he is also an Adept," said Zanos when Astra told him what she and Javik had Read. "Of course—when you told me he was Serafon's son, I should have guessed. No wonder he has amassed such power—and no wonder he's been planning to get out of the empire. He was afraid someone would discover his powers—just as I was."

"Someone did," said Astra.

"Who?"

"Portia," she replied. "It all fits now, Zanos. I saw Vortius outside Portia's office the day before you and I met—but it wasn't the first time he was there. I know I Read him at least once before, but thought nothing of it. Portia thought I knew more, though—such as that Vortius was keeping her alive and healthy with his powers!"

"He's a destroyer, Astra, not a healer."

"You use your powers both ways—why shouldn't he? Portia knew his secret—each had a hold on the other. And—by the gods, they plotted to kill me! Remember how sick I was, when you dared to heal me? Zanos, I've never been so ill from a sore throat—but Portia sought to rid herself of me and my wild Reading, because I had accidentally Read too many of her secrets. And Vortius certainly had no scruples about killing someone who might reveal him."

"Mm-hmm," said Zanos, nodding. "Ard saw you

go into Morella's the day you got sick. He reported it
to me, but he must also have reported it to Vortius—he
might even have conjured up that rainstorm!"

"Blessed gods—everything fits! When Portia attacked me the day of the games, I fought for my life,
and I hurt her badly. She must have sent for Vortius
to heal her! I've never believed that out of the kind-
ness of his heart he let you have a night to celebrate
before he claimed you. He'd have been right there
after the games if he hadn't been called to heal
Portia. He probably needed her help to distract some
of the Readers so he could make his escape—I'm
sure he simply would have let her die if he thought
he no longer needed her."

"Yes," Zanos agreed. "And now he's plotting even
more deaths. First he will take Lilith's castle, then
he will find a way to get other people into his power—
I've got to stop him!"

"Revenge?" Astra demanded.

"No! Well, yes, that too—but my wife, surely you
can see that Vortius has to be stopped before he
gains a strong base of operations such as Lilith's
lands!"

"And at least one Master Reader to aid him," she
said thoughtfully. "From what I saw of Amicus, he'll
go over to Vortius' side the moment he finds it
expedient. It's a good thing Vortius can't Read—for if
he found that out and added a powerful Reader to his
band of minor Adepts, we'd have no chance against
him at all."

"We?" asked Zanos.

"You don't think I'd let you go without me, do
you? After all the lessons in swordsmanship you've
put me through?"

Trel, Javik, and Kimma also insisted on going along,
as did every able-bodied person left alive in the
Settlement. To avoid having the watchers report them
as mysterious and potentially dangerous strangers,

they disguised themselves as traveling entertainers. Most of the villagers could sing and do folk dances well enough to get by, for Zanos and Astra's music was to be the star attraction.

Kimma demonstrated a wild and sultry dance guaranteed to mesmerize the country lads, while Javik came up with a spectacular juggling act with knives and swords—the rationale for traveling players to carry warriors' weapons.

When the Dark Moon Reader demonstrated, sending three razor-sharp knives spinning in an arc—adding a fourth—and a fifth—Astra realized that while he concentrated, he became unReadable.

With a flick of his wrist, Javik sent all five knives thunking into the tree stump in a perfect pattern. Then he picked up two swords, tossed one into the air—and caught it on the other, balancing tip to tip!

As he stood balancing the swords, Astra asked, "Aren't you afraid the audience will guess that you're using Adept power?"

Without missing a beat, Javik grinned at her. "In *these* lands, it doesn't matter. Everybody's used to minor Adepts. I'm copying a circus act I saw as a boy, inside the empire." He tossed the swords into the air and caught one in each hand. "When you do it as a performance, everyone assumes it's faked."

"Javik," said Zanos, "why didn't you tell us you have Adept powers? We've heard about people having both—"

"They're not two different powers," Javik replied. "It's what we're trained to. I was about ten, still in the Academy, when we went to the circus as a special outing. I was so impressed with the juggler that I borrowed some knives out of the kitchen and tried to copy his act . . . and I could. I was having a great fun till Master Solaris caught me—and he beat me as I had never been punished for any other prank, telling me how terribly dangerous it was, that I could have put out an eye, hurt the other boys—

"And all the time he was punishing me, I could Read the sick fear he felt for me. Believe me, I was impressed! At the time, I believed it was exactly what he said, that I could have hurt myself or one of the other boys.

"It was years later, when I observed people with minor Adept powers, that I realized that Master Solaris had recognized what I was really doing, even though I didn't know. But because it stopped my experiments, that beating probably saved my life.

"I really can't do much," he added. "Affecting the path of something in motion is my best trick. I can't start anything moving heavier than a leaf or a feather, can't control fire, and—much as I've prayed for the power—can't heal. But I've deflected enough knives and arrows over the years to be grateful for what powers I've got."

Their packing was soon complete. Ready to move out the next day, they ran through one final rehearsal. Javik had just done his juggling. Astra and Zanos sat on the tree stump to play for the folk dancing—when suddenly Astra clapped her hands to her head and cried out in pain.

Zanos dropped his flute and took her in his arms, looking to Javik for an explanation. The Dark Moon Reader stared at Astra, and winced. "Tiberium!" he said.

"Earthquake!" Astra gasped. Then she began to shout, "Get out of the forum! Run! The city will fall! All Readers—run for your lives!"

"Astra!" Zanos shook her, trying to break her free of the unseen influence. "Let go, Astra—stop Reading!"

But she moaned, sweat beading her face, her mind caught in some distant horror. Then she gave a despairing cry and went limp in his arms.

As Zanos was trying to rouse her, the earth shook.

In the Settlement it was no more than a vibration, as of a herd of horses galloping by. But in Tiberium—

Astra opened weary eyes, but Zanos was relieved that at least she was now looking at him. Then she looked over at Javik. "You Read?"

He nodded. "Part of it—but I was able to withdraw."

"What happened?" Zanos demanded.

"They were trying to save Tiberium from the earthquake," said Astra, "but—oh, Zanos, hundreds of people died!"

"They—the savage alliance?"

"Yes. Lenardo, Aradia, Lilith—all their allies. There is no question about it: their intentions were to *save* Tiberium—but they could not avert the prophecy."

"But . . . the prophecy was about the eclipse, and that's not till Summer Festival."

"No," she replied, shaking her head sadly. "The moon was the Dark Moon; the sun was the symbol of the Emperor and his family—including Portia. The whole royal family perished. Portia and Marina are dead. The senate was in an emergency session concerning corruption in the Academy system—and the whole building collapsed on them! Zanos . . . I have just witnessed the fall of the Aventine Empire!"

Even Zanos, who had so hated the country that had held him captive, felt a twinge of sadness. And for Astra it had been home, the land of her birth. He held her, and let her tell him of what she had witnessed, purge herself of the terrible details of her homeland's destruction.

The Emperor had been reviewing his troops in preparation for another assault against the savages. Lenardo and his cohorts were spread the length of the empire, trying to ease the strain on the underground fault which ran right down its center. To aid them, they had recruited hundreds of Dark Moon Readers—people dissatisfied enough to listen to the strangers, and willing to aid in saving their homeland when they were shown the genuine danger.

Until the actual event.

Lenardo's astonishing powers had not only pulled Astra into the rapport; they had united all those hundreds of Readers into one group mind. Through the Master Reader's powers they had Read the proof of betrayal—and taken their revenge, using the mind-blind Adepts they guided not to ease the fault, but to set it off, centering on Tiberium—crumbling the buildings around the forum, destroying the senate, pouring out their hatred for Portia—attacking everyone they blamed for their circumstances—

"And hundreds of innocent people as well," Astra finished bleakly. "Citizens. Common soldiers." She shivered, although the day was warm.

"So Tiberium is no more," said Zanos. "Serafon—"

"No," Astra said quickly. "No, Zanos—the worst destruction was all there around the forum. I could Read the struggle—but Lenardo and Aradia confined the damage, even if they could not avert it. Most of Tiberium was just shaken up, not destroyed. I will go out of body and Read for Serafon."

"But you were Reading directly a few minutes ago."

"Through the power of that gigantic rapport," she replied. "It's gone now, dissolved back into its individual parts. Let me Read now—in a few days' travel we will be too far from Tiberium for me to Read it, even out of body."

To Zanos' relief, Astra reported that the Temple of Hesta still stood, that the priestesses were taking in the injured and the homeless . . . and that Serafon lived, and was quietly applying healing powers along with bandages.

"But who now rules in Tiberium?" asked Trel, who had listened with the rest of the villagers in shocked silence.

"The alliance," replied Astra. "Or they will soon.

Conquest wasn't their intent, Trel—but they can't leave the country leaderless."

"But they've left their own lands unprotected!"

"I know," said Astra. "They thought all the Lords Adept would go right home after the fault was eased. Instead—"

"Instead it now looks as if they attacked the empire!" said Trel. "Once the news reaches their neighbors to the north, those Lords Adept will arm themselves, thinking that after the alliance has conquered all the lands to the south, it will start looking in the opposite direction."

"And they may decide to strike first," said Javik, "while the alliance has its energies dispersed."

"And if Vortius takes Lilith's castle," added Zanos, "that will be a sure sign that the alliance has spread itself too thin—an invitation to attack!"

"Then let's move!" said Astra.

Despite the lateness of the day, they did, traveling until well after dark, Astra and Javik Reading for the news to reach this far.

But even by morning it hadn't. The watchers reported the same innocuous events as always—including now the movements of a troupe of entertainers.

At midmorning they arrived in a village on market day. Despite their desire to forge northward, they had to act their parts—and their performance was such a success that the coins thrown at them were enough to buy another horse!

Most of their group was afoot, the only horses being Javik's and the ones Zanos and Astra had brought. The White Crow had stolen the rest. Now, however, they saw the chance to mount everyone and move faster.

So their performance in a small town that evening was even more enthusastic; they netted enough to buy food and two more horses, and their reputation began to precede them. Astra laughingly reported the watchers advising their fellows to trade duty time with those who hadn't heard yet, and go see the show.

It was difficult to rest nights when they wanted to reach Lilith's castle before Vortius struck—yet they would be in no condition to fight if they traveled both day and night, stopping only to perform.

At least this way they could move freely on the main road. They were greeted at each new community by children running out to meet them, eager to see the phenomenon they'd heard so much about.

And still no word came out of Tiberium—not even a report of savage victory.

They were now beyond Astra's ability to Read to Tiberium, even out of body. She could still Read to the Aventine border, where the guards accepted orders from their commanders to let no one in or out—

Until official word arrived that the savage alliance had put down an insurrection of the officers of the army. Now the army, too, was in the hands of the alliance; the border gates were opened, and news began to trickle out.

The traveling entertainers drove their horses all that day, knowing the watchers' messages would catch up and then pass them. By the next day, they did—and the troupe were able to skirt around communities too busy celebrating their rulers' latest victory to wonder what had happened to the entertainment they'd been awaiting.

But Lilith's people were no fools—they knew the dangers of living in a border territory—and when the happy news of victory also brought the information that their Lady Adept and her son were several days' ride away, they put their citizen-army on alert pending their leaders' safe return.

Zanos was fascinated. There was only a small standing army, with a disproportionate number of officers. But when the alert was called, an officer or two went to each nearby community, and all the able-bodied citizens spent part of each day drilling . . . but had the rest of their time to tend to their normal duties.

Vortius' army was also on the alert. Astra Read that it had grown a little, and the watchers—now sending scouts beyond the border, since they knew Lilith's enemies would be watching for signs of vulnerability—located the massed troops and sent a message speeding southward as fast as the flashes of light could flicker from one lookout to another.

Vortius also had scouts. Before Lilith's troops could gather to defend her castle he set out—using Adept power to kill the watchers who would have reported his movements.

Vortius' army was less than half a day's ride to the north of the castle, Zanos, Astra, and their friends about an equal distance to the south. Perhaps seventy of Lilith's soldiers in all were within distance to reach the castle before Vortius did—but once inside they might be able to hold it until further help came.

Without the watchers' warnings, though, they didn't know that the situation had become critical.

For once in her life, Astra blessed the extended range of her Reading talent as she reached out to Amicus. He was Reading, too—and trying to determine which side was stronger before throwing his lot in with them.

//You fool!// Astra projected to him. //Don't you know that Seriak is really Vortius?//

//Who—? Ah, you are the other Reader I've sensed spying—but not out of body any longer.// He Read Astra, Zanos, the others. //Who are you, renegade?//

//Magister Astra, of Portia's Academy,// she replied. //But Portia is dead now, and so is the corruption among Readers. Warn the castle that enemies are preparing to attack!//

//Why should I? These people took me hostage. I owe them nothing.//

//Then protect your own life! If Vortius wins, he'll either kill you or force you to do his will.//

//And what will *you* do if you win? Vortius has no Readers. He will reward me well for my services.//

To her horror, Astra realized that her intrusion had caused Amicus to choose sides—the wrong side!

She tried again. //Vortius might have bribed Readers in the empire—but out here he doesn't have to bother with the appearance of a good citizen. Amicus, he'll—//

The door to Amicus' room burst open. He turned to face a man in Lilith's livery, carrying a sword.

"Die, traitor!" the man cried, and, catching the Reader in utter surprise, plunged the sword into his heart.

Amicus' mind screamed with pain, assaulting Astra and striking down Master Corus' mental barriers.

//Amicus, what—?// "Guards! Guards! Help—we're being attacked!" Corus cried as he pounded on the door of his room.

But there was only one guard on duty—and he had just killed one of his charges. Now he turned to the other.

The second Reader fought valiantly, but, weaponless, he was no match for the guardsman's youth and strength. He was driven into a corner and slaughtered.

Although she could hardly cling to her horse amid the shared pain, Astra forced herself to continue Reading the scene. That guard—he was the same one Vortius had caused to choke on his scouting mission, and then provided "medicine" for! Now he was carrying out the orders Vortius had carefully programmed into him with subsequent doses of "medication," the last few doled out on secret trips out of the castle and paid for with detailed descriptions of floor plans and security routines.

At the news that reports had ceased from the watchers to the north, this man had first come up here to kill the Readers lest they give the alarm.

Astra realized that Vortius would never trust a Reader he couldn't control by some means other than a bribe. After all, someone else might offer a bigger reward!

Now the guard went quickly down to the courtyard and up the watchtower, where the man on duty turned anxiously to say, "I can't get any response from Yakov, sir!"

"I'll take over here," replied Vortius' man. "Go to the arms room and help prepare the weaponry."

"Aye, sir!"

Alone on the tower, the guard first faced northward, to where the next relay of watchers lay dead, where Vortius waited for his signal. "All is accomplished. Come ahead."

Then he turned to the south and flashed, "Cancel alert. No trouble here. Yakov's relief late. Tell Lilith all is well. Drav."

And remembering Drav's reaction the day Vortius had come to scout the castle, Astra was sure he was one of Lilith's most conscientious retainers. She would trust his word . . . and not hurry home.

Astra relayed what she had Read to her companions. "We have no choice—if we don't help defend that castle, Vortius will take it by nightfall."

"And get more people into his power—the most resistant ones with white lotus." Zanos shuddered, and urged his horse to a faster pace.

Now their problem was twofold: to warn the castle that Vortius was coming, and to persuade those who defended it that they were friends, not enemies.

That problem was still unresolved when they approached a roadblock set up by the army. "Where are you going?" demanded the officer in charge.

"To the Lady Lilith's castle," replied Trel. "We're entertainers, come to help celebrate the great victory over the Aventines."

"Sir," spoke up one of the soldiers, "I saw them

perform two days ago over at the Crossroads. They put on a fine show."

Astra Read the officer thinking that over. Word had just come from the watchers that the alert was a false alarm—Drav's counterfeit message.

"Very well," said the officer. "Pass through. Perhaps we'll be let off duty tonight and can see your show."

"Why are you blocking the road?" asked Trel. "Is there some danger ahead?"

"Nay—we thought there might be, but it proved merely a watcher late to his duties. We ought to be moving back toward the castle—if there *were* any trouble, that'd be the target." And Astra Read thoughts of Lilith's treasure rooms—certainly Vortius' target.

"Or *we* might be," Trel improvised quickly.

"Eh?" questioned the officer.

"We had a scare back there—all this activity has the bandit clans restless, you know."

"Aye—we've been having trouble with 'em south o' here ever since the Aventine invasion," agreed the officer. "You see something?"

"Aye. You know, we've picked up a nice bit of money our last few performances—generous folks 'round these parts," said Trel. "We're thinking of staying in this kingdom—my life's ambition has been to build my own theater, and I understand there is none in this country. But a bunch of bandits tried to ambush us this morning—there wasn't enough of them, and they quick gave up when they saw we'd fight for what's ours."

"But you're thinking, if you settle in these parts, are you going to have to defend yourselves—or will the Lady of the Land protect you? She will, sir—that I can promise as her loyal follower these twenty years. And for the rest of your journey—why don't you ride with us back to the castle? No bandits are going to attack a troop of Lady Lilith's army!"

It was exactly what Astra had had no idea of how

to accomplish. The officer, whose name was Brodik, was about the same age as Trel, and in half an hour the two men were fast friends. Kimma, and even Seela, flirted gently with some of the men, and they rode at a steady pace which Astra saw would put them near the castle at about the same time Vortius' troops arrived.

They were still far outnumbered, and she feared that there would not be time to get inside the castle and bar the gate against the invaders—but they had brought twenty armed and well-trained men to join forces with Lilith's retainers. Of the people in the castle, she could Read none in league with Drav— but he still manned the watchtower, relaying false messages that all was well, supposedly coming from the lookout post where Vortius had killed Yakov. The two guards he had sent for a break had resumed their posts outside Amicus' and Corus' rooms, with no idea that their charges now lay dead inside.

Zanos rode steadily, with the tension she recognized as the fighter's pitch, ready to move at the first threat. He had nothing to say—perhaps because some of the soldiers riding beside their little troupe might hear.

Wishing he could Read, she reached across and put her hand on his. He looked over and gave her an encouraging smile—and she knew he thought she was frightened.

And for the first time, she realized she wasn't.

No—it wasn't that she had no fear. Indeed, her stomach knotted when she thought that she might be killed, or Zanos might—and surely not all of their new friends could escape unscathed from the upcoming battle.

But it was a different kind of fear from the anxiety she had known all her life. She had made a choice— and she had absolutely no fear that it was wrong! Even if Vortius won, she still knew she would have no doubt that she had chosen right. Her self-doubts were gone.

So she squeezed Zanos' hand. "I'm all right," she said. "No matter what happens, I'm all right—and I love you."

"As I love you," he replied. "We're going to win, Astra—we'll get rid of Vortius, and then you and I are going to have a long and happy life together."

And she Read that his desire for vengeance, if not gone, was outweighed by his concern and love for her. She sent out her own thoughts, even if he could not Read them—and the look in his blue eyes told her that he understood enough without Reading—

The moment was shattered by an outcry ahead, and the sound of galloping horses. Astra Read the castle, which was now just up the steep road they were climbing, the watchtower already in view.

The road from the north converged with this one near the castle gates—and someone had seen from a castle window Vortius' unreported army approaching!

Two men swarmed up to the watchtower, looked out—and one of them grabbed up the horn and blew a mighty blast as the other shook Drav, demanding, "What's the matter with you? Why didn't you sound the alarm?!" Then he flung Drav down the ladder, where he lay stunned for a moment—then drew his knife and started to throw it at his attacker. But the other guard flung a spear from the tower, and Drav was dead.

"Close the gates!" shouted one of the guards—but the other grasped his arm and pointed toward Brodik's troop approaching from the south, bearing the banners with Lilith's blue lion.

"*Guard* the gates!" came the revised order. "Let the troops in, but keep out the attackers!"

Easier said than done. By this time, Brodik was aware that something was happening at the castle—he had heard the horn, and Astra couldn't be sure, since she had Read them, whether the guards' instructions were audible from here.

They all spurred their horses—but so did Vortius

and his troops, arriving at almost the same time where the two roads widened into a sort of plaza before the castle gates.

The first of Brodik's trained soldiers spread themselves in a diagonal from the gate across the northern road, allowing everyone else to ride into the castle behind their barrier—giving their lives blocking the way of the attackers, but taking a sizeable number with them into death.

The troupe from the Settlement and Brodik's surviving soldiers leaped down from their horses. "Bar those gates!" Brodik shouted as people swarmed up onto the castle walls and began to rain arrows down on the attackers.

Zanos had not seen Vortius in the attacking army, but of course he would not expose himself in the front ranks. Nor had he come unprepared for barred gates.

The moment Zanos climbed up to the platform from which he could look over the wall, he saw a battering ram being moved up from the rear of Vortius' entourage. Men in armor heavy enough to deflect arrows slowly hauled the heavy instrument forward, up against the gate, where they shoved blocks under its wheels, then wound the thing back with pulleys to the limit of the straps it hung in. The armored point hit the gates with a splintering thud, but they held. The first time.

Arrows and spears had little effect on the armored men winding the instrument back for a second blow. Zanos tried to stop the heart of one of the men—but he was moving, the target too hard to concentrate on. Although he staggered, his misstep was not enough to stop the progress of the battering ram.

Then he remembered something Mallen had done against him. He concentrated on the man's armor, thinking of the metal parts being hot as iron in a forge, burning through the padding beneath—

His victim screamed and dropped out of his place, tearing at his armor—and Zanos looked to the man next to him, trying the same technique.

But it was too slow—and by the time the second man leaped away from his task, the first was back at his despite his smarting burns.

The ram was a log as thick as a man was tall, solid, and freshly cut, heavy with sap. There was no hope of setting it aflame—

And as Zanos was still pondering some way to keep the gates from being battered down, the ram struck a second time—and the center of the gates splintered, knocking the heavy bar halfway across the courtyard.

With a mighty cheer, Vortius' troops charged around the battering ram and into the yard.

Zanos turned, looking for Astra—but before he could find her he was faced with two men climbing the ladder to the platform, trying to get at him. It was a permanent ladder—he couldn't kick it over—but it was easy enough to kick the first man in the face, knocking him down on top of his fellow.

They were both up by the time Zanos leaped to the ground, but they were semitrained, hacking and slashing at him and wasting their strength. He slid easily in under one man's guard for a slash to the thigh that left him lying gasping in pain. The other had a potbelly. His breastplate, obviously stolen from armor designed for a thinner man, rode high—and Zanos skewered him through the middle, jumping back as his guts spewed forth when he pulled out the sword.

Still, he could not see Astra! The courtyard was filled with fighting, the castle's defenders being driven back by the sheer numbers of attackers. More poured through the gateway every moment.

Slashing right and left, ever alert for attack from behind, Zanos started to work his way to the center of the courtyard, hoping to find his wife.

But it was not Astra he found when a woman's cry of anguish made him turn—it was Lanna!

Ard was clumsily slashing at one of Brodik's soldiers—and Lanna saw that he was outmatched. She leaped on his opponent, clawing at his eyes, and with that moment's advantage Ard managed to run the man through . . . only to turn and face vengeance incarnate.

"Zanos!" he gasped.

Lanna looked up, and went pale as death.

"You betrayed me," said Zanos. "You sold me out, just as I was about to free you. If Vortius had drugged you, I would have understood—but you acted of your own free will!"

"Zanos, no!" Ard pleaded. "How could we refuse to do what Vortius wanted? With all his power—?"

"His power can be defeated by people who work together!" Zanos shouted.

"But he's got a whole army!" Lanna pleaded. "Zanos—he'll forgive you. Don't hurt us—come work with us for Vortius—"

Their group was causing an eddy in the fighting. As Zanos lifted his sword to dispatch Ard—who was making no attempt to defend himself—he was hit from the side by several fighters toppled by another group—

And before he could recover and reach him, Ard was clubbed by another fighter, while Lanna, screaming, "Ard!" was dragged off by three men, and disappeared into the melee.

Zanos stopped only long enough to see that Ard was dead. Then he tried to follow Lanna through the mass of struggling humanity.

He found Kimma holding off two brutes with her short sword, and stepped in to take one of them off her hands. "Thanks!" she snapped—and used the feint she had showed him to rid herself of her opponent, while Zanos easily slashed the throat of the other, who had lost the neckpiece to his helmet.

"Kimma, where did Astra—?" Zanos shouted over the clanging of swords.

But just then, Brodik saw Kimma. "Hey, girl! All women and wounded take shelter in the dungeon—now!"

"I can fight as well as any man!" Kimma protested.

"Go!" said Zanos. "If Vortius' men break through, the other women will need your protection. Most of them *can't* fight!"

Kimma began working her way toward the entry to the castle. Zanos followed, assuming Astra had taken shelter with the other women. If only he could Read for her!

He could also not be sure how the battle was going. By sheer numbers, Vortius' men would win— but a strategic retreat into the castle might allow the defenders to hold out until help arrived. The watchers, receiving either no messages from the castle or word of the attack, would send out a call for all troops in this area to converge here. If Vortius didn't have the castle secured and ready to defend by that time, he would be defeated.

But Vortius' minor Adepts, who had apparently been saving their strength earlier, began to operate. Fires broke out in the castle, sending people fleeing from the smoke. Men dropped heated weapons, or fell dead of heart failure.

Zanos turned from his progress toward the door into the castle, certain that these events presaged the arrival of Vortius himself.

And indeed, through the splintered gates rode Vortius—surrounded by Zanos' gladiators!

He *knew* how loyal they were—just as loyal as he had been under the influence of white lotus. They would give their lives in defense of Vortius now.

Torn between finding Astra and facing Vortius, Zanos wavered for a moment—and then decided on a strategic retreat before Vortius knew he was here. He could not defeat six dedicated men whom he had trained himself! His only chance was to bide his time and take Vortius by surprise.

So he fought his way to the door into the castle, which was guarded well—but one of Brovik's soldiers recognized him, and he was allowed in. "I'm going down to help protect the women and wounded," he announced.

"Good work," replied the man. "We'll hold this door as long as possible—but it don't look good."

Zanos wound his way down narrow, torch-lit stairs until he came out in Lilith's dungeons. Here he found two pregnant women, several children, and all the wounded who had been able to get down those treacherous stairs. Kimma guarded them while the women of the castle dressed wounds, gave medication, and comforted those in pain.

Astra was bent over a man bleeding from a gut wound, the smell warning that he would die of infection without the aid of Adept healing.

Zanos stepped to his side, and put the man to sleep. Then, as Astra looked up at him wordlessly with her beautiful smile, he started healing heat to destroy the infection. At Astra's directions, he drew together the man's intestines, then the muscle over them, healing the wound from the inside out to a stage where his body would repair the rest while he lay sleeping.

Astra sat back on her heels with a sigh. "They keep coming. I'm afraid to Read the battle." But she did, he could tell, as her eyes took on a faraway look. "Help is coming! But they're far away yet—and Vortius is nearing the door into the castle."

"He has no reason to come down here," said Zanos. "You'll be safe."

"Oh, but he has *good* reason," Astra replied. "Come and look."

She led him along a narrow passageway cut deep into the bowels of the mountain. Light faded, but flickered up ahead when they turned a corner. It was cold and dank here. Puddles of stagnant water pooled on the stone floor. A single torch lit the way.

At the very end of the passage, a sturdy door stood—locked, of course. "Any Adept can open it," said Astra, "but no one else. The mechanism is on the inside—lift the lever directly behind here," she pointed, "and it will be unlocked."

Zanos unlocked the door, and Astra pushed it open to reveal—

Chests upon chests, most of them closed, but several open to reveal gold rings, gold and silver coins, precious stones—

"Lilith's treasure!" Zanos exclaimed. "By Mawort—if Vortius can't hold the castle, he can buy himself an army big enough to take the whole territory if he can carry all this away!"

"And Drav was an officer of Lilith's guards. Vortius surely made him tell where the treasure is kept. So he will fight his way down here if he possibly can."

Zanos took a deep breath of anticipation. "Excellent," he said. "The perfect bait to bring the enemy into my trap!"

Astra stared at Zanos as she pulled shut the door to the treasure room. He was unReadable, automatically set to use Adept power at the thought of wreaking vengeance on Vortius. It sent a chill down her spine—and yet what could she do? He could never rest until he had met his nemesis, face to face.

So she said, "How can we lay a trap that will actually capture him? Besides you and Kimma and me, we have no one down here capable of fighting."

"Lilith's soldiers will fight all the way, protecting helpless people as well as the treasure," Zanos replied. "But you're right—we could certainly use a few more good fighters. Can you contact Javik?"

"He's on his way here now, with someone wounded," Astra replied. "But I'll tell him—" Quickly, she relayed the situation to the Dark Moon Reader, and as

he worked his way through the fighting in the castle
hallway, he located Trel and told him the plan. The
old man, blood-spattered and still fighting strongly,
began shouting to what villagers he could spot. Brodik
heard, and directed several soldiers to retreat to the
dungeon—and they helped Javik carry the casualty
he had found down the treacherous stairs.

It was a woman, severely beaten—and raped. It
sickened Astra to Read what had been done to her,
but she set that aside as she knelt beside her. "Zanos—
her spleen is ruptured—she's bleeding to death!"

Even so, the woman came to—and the moment
she was conscious Astra recognized her despite her
distorted features. "Lanna!"

"No! No!" the woman moaned, her head thrashing
as Astra Read flashes of memory that told her several
of Vortius' men had wanted the pretty young woman,
but she had remained faithful to Ard, creating jealousy that had erupted today—

Lanna's eyes focused. She looked past Astra to
Zanos, and her heart pumped violently in terror.
"No—not you—"

And she passed out as her life's blood pumped
away.

"Zanos!" shouted Astra.

"I'm trying!" he replied. "Astra—*where* must I
stop the bleeding?"

But it was too late. Lanna was dead—and trying to
pump her heart back to life would only force broken
ribs to pierce her lungs. Astra stared at Zanos. "You
let her die! I know she betrayed you, but—"

"No!" he exclaimed. "Astra, I wanted to kill her—
not torture her! You can't think I'd do that to any
woman!"

"No," she whispered. "I'm sorry."

More soldiers were coming down to the dungeon,
bringing more wounded. Astra worked, Zanos at her
side, concentrating on what she was doing right
there—until finally there was not another mangled

limb to set or wound to close. But soldiers were pouring down the stairs.

Followed by Vortius' men. They seemed to flow in like a river, three and four against every defender, cutting down villagers and Lilith's men, trampling over the bodies.

And behind them came Vortius, surrounded by four of Zanos' gladiators—the other two lay dead, Astra found, in the corridor above.

Three soldiers swarmed over Kimma—but at the same time four more threatened Javik! Zanos tried to take two of them off the Reader while Astra drew her sword to assist Kimma.

More men came, overwhelming them.

Kimma went down.

On her back, she still struck upward with her sword, gutting one of them, who fell screaming—but his fellow ran his sword through her throat and she fell back, dead.

Not knowing even that she did it, Astra picked up Kimma's sword with her left hand. She now had a short sword in either hand, and, as in improvising a dance, she slashed one way and then the other at her attackers, whirling, leaping—catching one in the throat, another in the belly, pirouetting in spilled blood to slice the laces holding the breastplate of the man attacking her next, then reversing her swing to slash his belly open, spilling guts.

She was wide open to Reading, living every life in that dungeon—and dying every death.

Javik was forced backward over the bodies of fallen soldiers. He fell—Zanos could not disengage from the man he was fighting—Astra whirled and struck Javik's opponent from behind, her sword clattering off his armor, but making him miss his blow at Javik.

//Thanks!// Javik told her—but it was for naught. The man he had fallen on was still alive. Both Astra and Javik Read him pull a knife—but Javik was still off-balance. He twisted, but slipped in blood, could not avoid the blow—

And the man stabbed him through the heart.

At the same moment, Astra drove her sword into Javik's killer's throat, but it was too late—the Reader's death agony rang in her mind, heating it to fury.

Now it was Astra and Zanos against Vortius and the four gladiators. The soldiers were all dead or critically wounded. A huge black man charged Zanos. Astra Read that although Zanos had far more skill, the other had the sheer brute strength to endure beyond her husband's capabilities after expending so much Adept power.

And Vortius had used little or none!

"Stop his heart!" she cried to Zanos.

She meant Vortius—but it was the black man who gagged and dropped like a felled ox.

The other three gladiators charged at once. Astra felt Zanos become Readable—knew that it meant his strength was wavering. Why had she expected him to help her with healing the wounded? They would all die now anyway, because he hadn't the strength left to combat Vortius!

Zanos and Astra backed away, stumbling over the dead and the living, driven inexorably along the corridor leading to the treasure room. The light grew dim as they left the range of the torches in the infirmary area. One of the gladiators squinted, and Zanos ran him through.

Two on two—reasonable odds except that following behind came Vortius, letting his men tire out his prey, calling, "Give it up, Zanos. You can't win—but you can stay alive, you and your pretty little wife. It would be a shame to let my men kill her, you know. I won't even give her to them—at least not very often. I can use the services of a good Reader—I've missed that since Portia died."

The light brightened as they rounded the curve into the narrow hallway near the treasure room—and the flickering torchlight gave Astra an idea. "Take them, Zanos!" she exclaimed—and as he engaged the man attacking her as well as his own, she whirled and with her right-hand sword slashed the burning top off the torch, plunging them all into darkness as it fell to the dank floor and rolled into a puddle.

In the dark, she Read, leaped, struck—one gladiator—the second—

Now Vortius—

Light returned just as she started toward him—he had used his powers to light the stub of the torch left in the holder. It wasn't as bright as the oil-fed flame, but it was sufficient.

Astra was standing in front of Zanos. He grasped her wrist and pulled her back. "Vortius is mine," he told her.

"Zanos, you are a fool," said Vortius. "You have expended your powers—you can't win against me."

And Astra felt pain clench at Zanos' heart.

He gasped—but fought it off. The fancy tabard Vortius wore over his armor burst into flame—but he simply stood there laughing, letting it burn away to nothing.

Zanos launched himself at Vortius with his sword—but the man was wearing perfectly fitting armor with no chinks to let a sword through where it could do any good. Only his arms and legs were vulnerable—and when Zanos slashed at his thigh the sword was easily deflected.

Zanos, you can't win that way! thought Astra. Her husband was playing Vortius' game. *Make him play your game!* But there was no use saying it aloud—she had no idea of how to force Vortius to do so.

But Zanos was too experienced a fighter to continue ineffective tactics. He was panting—gathering air into his blood while he rested for a moment, letting Vortius talk. "Why don't you just give it up, Zanos? You know you can't win. Just give me your sword, and tell your wife to give me hers. Then you can help me carry the treasure back to camp before Lilith's army gets here."

The gambler laughed. "Did you think you could stall for time until they got here? Oh, no—I have *my* watchers, too, my friends. You've cost me six fine bodyguards this day, Zanos—so you're going to have to do their work for them. Don't worry—I'll give you white lotus again. Remember how good it feels? You'll have no worries, no guilt over this silly little escapade. What did you hope to gain, anyway? All Lady Lilith would have done was force you into *her* service—so what's the difference?"

As the gambler stepped forward, Zanos projected, //Astra—get behind him.//

But Vortius was not to be caught that easily. The moment Astra began to edge to the side, he whirled to face her. "Oh, no, my dear—we don't—"

Zanos struck low, slicing through Vortius' thigh—but the blood hardly trickled out, and Astra Read the wound close neatly up again as Vortius said angrily, "We'll have to teach you a lesson, won't we?" He held out his hand, and Zanos' diaphragm constricted—he couldn't breathe, and he couldn't seem to shake it off!

Astra, though, grasped the chance to strike at Vortius' outstretched arm—at that moment she would have been glad to cut it off, but that was far beyond her strength. Still, she produced a deep cut, and while Vortius was concentrating on healing himself, Zanos recovered.

"What is this?" demanded Vortius. "Do you think to pester me to death with gnat bites?"

Astra's dress burst into flame!

She gasped—but had the presence of mind to drop and roll in the water on the floor, bouncing to her feet soggy but unhurt.

"Master—where are you?" came a voice from around the turn in the corridor.

"In here, men!" called Vortius—and Astra Read

seven more of Vortius' troops coming along the corridor.

It was over. They couldn't possibly hold out against seven more men and Vortius!

Unless—

"Zanos—!" she began—but Vortius' powers clutched at her throat now, preventing her from getting out //The torches! Put out all the torches!//

The one by the treasury was still flickering—but now, as if Zanos had somehow deduced her thought, it went out. So did the ones along the corridor. The oncoming soldiers stumbled in the dark—

And Zanos leaped on Vortius as if he could see or Read him, knocking him down, tearing at his armor— and plunging his knife into the gambler's throat! The grip on Astra was released, and she coughed as she drew air deep into her lungs.

Vortius fought with all his strength—but they had made him use his powers in healing himself, and now as he tried to close his throat wound Zanos twisted the knife, kneeling on Vortius' chest, slashing and slashing until all the life went out of the man's body, and he lay limp, Zanos bending forward on top of him, strength gone.

A flare of light—someone had relit one of the torches. Seven soldiers came around the corridor to see their leader dead, Zanos kneeling over him, Vortius' blood on his hands—

"Get 'im!"

Astra tried to meet them, wielding her two swords, but they stopped short. She could take one at a time in the narrow corridor—and she could Read that they knew if she had stayed alive this long, she had to be dangerous.

The configuration shifted—the best swordsman among them moved forward to meet Astra. "Zanos," she called—but he remained where he was. Did she have to defend him alone?

No—the hilt of the sword in her opponent's hand

grew too hot to handle—he dropped it, but the next man pushed past him and struck at her, only to drop, clutching his chest. Zanos slumped atop Vortius, almost unconscious.

"Give up!" Astra told the others, hoping to keep them from noticing how exhausted Zanos was. "Give up and we'll let you live. Vortius is dead—you owe him no further loyalty!"

"Well, we'll just take a bunch o' that there treasure and go out on our own!" replied one of the men. "Lessee here—*you* ain't the Adept—it's *him*!"

And he raised the spear he carried and flung it with all his strength straight at Zanos—

In that split-instant Astra Read that Zanos had no strength left—he could not even move! She saw the weapon rushing straight at him—Read it through his weary eyes—felt a rush of heat exploding through her chest—

The spear wavered in its course, swerved—and missed Zanos by a hair's breadth!

And Astra fainted dead away.

Zanos came to in a room he didn't recognize, but he knew the face peering into his: Trel.

"So you've decided to come back to us, lad," said the old man.

Memory poured back—he might have been left for dead, but . . . "Astra!"

"She's all right, Zanos! But she's still sleeping."

"What happened?" Zanos asked, taking in his surroundings. He was on a pallet in what must be the great hall of the castle. Around him were many other pallets, where those who had been wounded in the battle slept.

"You and Astra defended the treasury to the last," Trel told him. "Brodik and I had to fight our way through Vortius' men to get down there after he thought he'd taken the place—we got there just in time. You barely deflected that spear, and it was too much for Astra—she just fainted dead away."

"What? When was this?" The light was wrong for it to be evening.

"Yesterday," Trel told him.

"Yesterday! Why is Astra still sleeping? What haven't you told me? She's not the kind of woman who faints! Was she wounded? Where is she?"

"We put all the women together in another room," Trel explained. "Zanos—I don't *know* why Astra hasn't wakened. She doesn't seem to be hurt. If you've got enough strength to walk, you can see her."

Zanos' knees felt like jelly, but he managed to walk with Trel ino the room where Astra lay sleeping. She didn't look injured. Her color was normal, she breathed regularly, and he could feel the pulse in her wrist. But she did not wake at his touch.

"By the gods, I wish I could Read!" said Zanos. "Trel, isn't there any other Reader—?"

"Javik is dead," the old man said sadly.

"Yes—he died bravely," replied Zanos. "But how am I to find out—?"

It was a hunch, or perhaps just a memory of the way Serafon had touched him to bring him out of healing sleep when he was wounded. Whatever the reason, Zanos gently placed a finger on Astra's forehead, between her eyes.

Her eyes fluttered open. //Zanos?// "Zanos?" It was like an echo, first the thought, then the word—

"Blessed gods!" he whispered.

//Where are we? Why can't—?// "Where are we, Zanos? I—Zanos, I can't Read!"

But he could—he felt her fear thrust through him like a sword wound. "It's all right!" he told her, gathering her into his arms. "Astra, you're all right— you just—"

He looked at Trel over Astra's shoulder. "You said . . . that I deflected a spear?"

"Yes," Astra answered, not knowing he was asking

Trel. "It must have taken the very last of your strength. Then—did someone hit me? How? I'm a Reader, but—"

Again he felt her panic. Trel said, "No one hit you, Astra. I came just in time to see what happened. Zanos deflected the spear, and then you passed out."

"You were there?" She seemed confused. "I don't understand. Why didn't I know you were there?"

"Astra," said Zanos, "you weren't Reading just then because I didn't deflect any spear. I remember now—I had no strength at all. I couldn't even duck. *You* deflected that spear, Astra—and you saved my life."

"But I can't—" she protested.

"Javik said it was all one power. Obviously he was right."

"And when he used his Adept power too much," added Trel, "it would affect his Reading. I remember the day we felled that big tree—the stump that stands in the middle of the Settlement. We wanted it to fall where we hadn't built any homes yet—in the area we were planning to expand into. We thought we had the cut just right, wedges in place, so when we knocked them out it would fall right where we wanted it—but none of us were experts at that craft, and something made it fall at the wrong angle. It would have hit three homes—but Javik deflected it in mid-air, so it fell where we wanted it. He couldn't Read after that for almost two days." He smiled encouragingly at Astra. "When he had those Reading losses, he was impossible to put up with. I suppose Zanos will have to learn to wait it out if it makes you as bad-tempered as it did Javik."

"Javik," whispered Astra, a tear trembling on the edge of her lashes. "Kimma. Oh, Trel—did anyone but you survive?"

"Most of the rest of us. Now, both you young people need something to eat, and then more sleep if I'm any judge.

It seemed to Astra that all she did was eat and sleep for the next several days. She and Zanos were given a room on one of the upper levels—but there was no temptation to do anything but sleep in the big soft bed.

They did go out once, for a funeral ceremony when all the bodies, friend and enemy, were burned on the common pyre. Unable to Read, Astra found it only confusing—except for one moment as, around the circle, people spoke out for those they had loved or respected. Trel spoke for Kimma and Javik, and Astra added, "I knew them only a short time, but I will miss them sorely."

"So shall I," said Zanos. "And . . . I must speak for Vortius. Today is a day to remember, not the wrongs he did, but rather that . . . the mother who mourns him is a dearly beloved friend."

Astra squeezed his hand, thinking that Serafon would be glad to know that her son's death did not go unremembered, as did those of Amicus and Corus.

With each day they needed less sleep, but Astra still found herself unable to keep awake after lunch. Zanos said it was because she refused meat, which would have given her strength back more quickly— but Astra was determined to give the Reading powers that had once been her bane every chance to return.

One day when she woke to a touch on her forehead, it was not Zanos' blue eyes she looked into, but bright eyes set into a wrinkled old face she had seen somewhere before—

//It's all right, child. I'm no more a traitor than you are.//

"Master Clement!" And then she realized, "I can Read again!"

"Yes, your powers should return to normal very soon. You're suffering a common aftereffect of a Reader's first use of Adept power. If you're feeling up to it, the Lady Lilith would like to meet with you and your husband."

She instinctively Read for Zanos, and found him in the great hall, now cleared of the injured, talking with two young men: one of them a lanky adolescent dressed in the richly embroidered garments of a young lord, the other the boy who had been with Master Clement in Tiberium that day she had met Zanos—how long ago it seemed, although it was less than a year! Decius—the boy who walked on a wooden leg, the one who had been defending Torio and Lenardo back when she had thought them all traitors—

There was so much to sort out. *Oh, Zanos, will we ever find the place where we belong?*

//Astra—you're awake!//

//What? Zanos—you—?//

//Your Reading's back! Wonderful! Come on, sleepyhead—everything's happening without you!//

Master Clement left Astra to dress, although she had napped in everything but her outer dress and shoes. Hastily she put them on, smoothed her hair, and hurried downstairs to join her husband.

"Why didn't you tell me you could Read?" she demanded. "When did it happen?"

"I'm sure of it since I woke up after the battle. But I think . . . Astra, do you remember when you told me to put out the torches?"

"Yes . . . no—I couldn't say it. Vortius was choking me!"

"But I heard you! I mean, at the time I thought I heard you—and then in the dark, Vortius was helpless, while I— It wasn't as if I could see him. I could just, uh, *sense* where he was and what he was doing."

"I understand," she replied. "Readers don't usually visualize—that's what we call actually seeing a scene when we're not there, or when it's too dark. Visualizing is very difficult, unless you're out of body." She gave a little laugh. "So we've learned each other's powers. But you've been practicing Reading, while I haven't dared to try using Adept powers again."

"I'll teach you," he said. "I used to use too much power at first, too—Serafon taught me how to control."

He introduced her to Decius and the other boy, Lilith's son, Lord Ivorn. Soon Master Clement came to take them to Lady Lilith's study.

The Lady Adept certainly belied anyone's notion of "savage." Her face was pale, cool, serene, her dark hair simply coiffed and surmounted by a small gold circlet. She wore a dress of blue satin embroidered in silver, and spoke in a straightforward, effective manner.

"Zanos and Astra, you do not even know me, and yet you have done me great service. How comes it that you should fight for my people, preserving my land and my treasures for their good?"

They did their best to explain under her scrutinizing eye, Astra wondering if this woman, too, was endowed with both powers. "And so," Zanos finished, "we simply could not allow Vortius, who has harmed so many, to gain a vantage point here in these lands which we have found to be ruled so peacefully and fairly."

Lilith glanced at Master Clement. "They speak the truth," he said.

"Zanos," continued Lilith, "you say you seek your homeland of Madura—yet you admit that it is unlikely to be the pleasant land that you remember. Do you have property or family there?"

"Property, no. Family—all dead, except my brother. When the slavers came, they killed our parents. We ran. I was caught. My brother escaped—I hope. If he still lives in Madura—"

"Of course," the Lady Adept replied. "You must go and see. But I must reward both of you for your service to me, and since you have powers in your own right, demonstrated by defeating an attacking force, by our traditions you deserve a portion of the lands you saved."

Astra shared Zanos' amazement. "You would offer *us*—? But you don't even *know* us!"

"I know you by your actions. And Master Clement agrees with me from what he has Read of you. It is my right to offer you a part of my lands—but if you accept, you must swear loyalty not only to me, but to the savage alliance—or the Savage Empire, as we now call it—and agree to rule in peace, to protect your people, not to exploit them, and to come to the aid of any member of the alliance who calls for your help."

Astra stared at the floor, and tried not to let her feelings reach out to Zanos. Oh, how she longed to cease from their wanderings, to make a home here, among these people who had accepted them—

"Astra." Her husband was looking into her eyes. "Astra, this must be *our* decision," he said.

"I—I promised that I would go with you to Madura," she told him.

"And I intend to go," he replied. "But my wife— from what we have heard, I do not think we will want to stay there. If we find my brother—if it is as much a land of evil as we have been told, we could have a home here to bring him to.

"Besides," he added softly, "we have good friends here now—and Serafon may be persuaded to come this far north, if not to the northern isles."

"Oh . . . Zanos!" she whispered. "Oh, yes, my husband!"

"Then it is agreed," Lilith told them with a smile. "One more thing—you will have to stay in your lands long enough to allow your people to know and trust you. Will you agree to a year before you set off on your search for your brother?"

"It has been more than twenty years," said Zanos. "If he lives . . . surely he will live for one year more."

When Astra and he were finally alone together in their room—and wide awake—he told her, "We now have the time and the security to consummate our marriage!"

"And recover afterward," she said with a laugh, "and I to learn how to use Adept powers, and you to Read." She kissed him—and then added, feeling the tolerant humor of Master Clement as he shut himself off from Reading what Zanos was broadcasting, "Oh, my—you'll have to learn how *not* to Read at the wrong time, if we're to have any privacy when there are other Readers about!"

"That's easy," he murmured into her ear, nibbling it—and the ties of her dress began unloosening of their own accord as her husband became blank to Reading.

"I wonder if I can do that—without fainting?" she said, and concentrated on the bow that held his shirt closed, as if she tugged at one of the ends—it moved! Astra laughed. "Zanos—that's the solution to my life-long problem! I don't have to have the whole world intruding on me if I don't want it!"

"That's good," he murmured distractedly against her hair. "Why don't you tell me all about it—tomorrow?"

The End

ABOUT THE AUTHORS

JEAN LORRAH is the creator of the *Savage Empire* series, in which *Flight to the Savage Empire* is the fourth book. The first three are *Savage Empire, Dragon Lord of the Savage Empire,* and *Captives of the Savage Empire.* She is coauthor with Jacqueline Lichtenberg of *First Channel* and *Channel's Destiny* in Jacqueline's Sime/Gen series, and has written a solo novel in that series, *Ambrov Keon.* She is also the author of the professional *Star Trek* novel *The Vulcan Academy Murders,* and coeditor with Lois Wickstrom of *Pandora,* a small-press sf magazine.

Jean has a Ph.D. in Medieval British Literature. She is Professor of English at Murray State University in Kentucky. Her first professional publications were nonfiction; her fiction was published in fanzines for years before her first professional novel was published in 1980. She maintains a close relationship with sf fandom, appearing at conventions and engaging in as much fannish activity as time will allow. On occasion, she has the opportunity to combine her two loves of teaching and writing by teaching creative writing.

WINSTON HOWLETT has a B.A. in Mass Communication. A former news writer, he is now a free-lance media producer and director. After writing dozens of stories and articles for fanzines, he made his first professional sale in 1978. He and Jean met through science fiction fandom, and occasionally appear on panels together at conventions. An electronic musician, Winston is planning an album of "spirit music" based on the *Savage Empire* series.